ALL YOU'LL EVER NEED

D1736630

SHARON C. COOPER

ALL YOU'LL EVER NEED

ISBN-13: 978-0-9903505-3-8

*Bestselling author Sharon C. Cooper brings you
another exciting romance…*

Dear Reader

I enjoy reading books that are a part of a series, and now I find that I enjoy writing them as well. Join me as I introduce you to a few members of the Jenkins family.

Steven Jenkins, the patriarch of the Jenkins family, and founder of Jenkins & Sons Construction wants what every entrepreneur head of the family wants - for his children to continue to run the family business long after he's dead and gone. None of his four sons and three daughters are interested in taking over the reins. It's not until his oldest granddaughter, Peyton Jenkins, shows an interest that his hope is renewed.

Now its 16 years later, he's happily retired, and business is better than ever - thanks to his five amazing granddaughters. Toni (TJ) Jenkins, a master plumber, is his favorite granddaughter - though he'll never admit it; Jada (JJ) Jenkins is the youngest and the most spirited of the bunch. Steven still hasn't been able to figure her out, but he has to admit, she's a darn good sheet metal worker. Then there's Christina (CJ) Jenkins, the shy one in the group and the most compassionate. She's a painter, but refers to herself as an artist. Martina (MJ) Jenkins, is a carpenter and Steven's most challenging grandchild who keeps everyone on their toes. Last, but not least, is sweet, levelheaded Peyton (PJ) Jenkins - an electrician and the senior construction manager for Jenkins & Sons Construction.

I hope you enjoy this installment of the Jenkins Family Series or as I like to think of them – the Jenkins clan.

Enjoy!
Sharon C. Cooper
www.sharoncooper.net

CHAPTER ONE

It is definitely raining men up in here. Jada Jenkins wove in and out of the small groups of people, stopping periodically to greet some of the guests at her cousin's wedding. She took special note of the handsome and hopefully single men hanging out near the bar at the reception.

"Girl, where did you find all of these gorgeous men?" Jada yelled over the deafening music pumping through the speakers a couple of feet away. She handed her cousin, Toni Jenkins, now Mrs. Toni Jenkins-Logan, a glass of ginger ale and claimed the seat next to her.

"You have Craig to thank for that." Toni sipped from her drink. She squinted and scrunched up her face. "Goodness this soda is strong." She took another small sip. "As for the gorgeous men, it turns out Craig has a lot of friends, and you'll be glad to know many of them are single."

"Hmm, that is good to know. I'll have to talk with my new cousin-in-law, but right now, I still can't believe you got married before me." Jada crossed her legs, a coral five-inch rhinestone embellished sandal dangled from her foot revealing the red bottom. "I'm the one who spends an arm and a leg making sure I look like someone from Life Styles of the Rich and Famous. Yet, you're the one who lands a Prince Charming. Hell, you didn't even want to get married."

Toni laughed. Her gaze landed on her new husband who stood across the banquet hall talking with the groomsmen. Jada didn't miss the way Toni's face lit up each time she glanced at Craig, and she couldn't ever remember seeing her cousin this happy.

"It's not that I didn't want to get married, I just thought I never would." Toni's gaze dropped to the table where she absently fingered a cloth napkin and then lifted her sparkling eyes to Jada. "This has been a long, exhausting day, but it has been one of the best days of my life. I'm so excited that I get to spend the rest of my days with the most amazing man I've ever met. It's like a dream. Add having his baby to the mix, and I feel as if I'm living someone else's fantasy."

Jada reached over and squeezed Toni's hand. She was happy for Toni, or TJ as most of the Jenkins family called her, but she couldn't help but be a little envious. TJ was three months pregnant after believing she could never have children, and now she had married cutie-pie Craig Logan, an all-around great guy who was madly in love with her cousin. Jada wondered if she ever would experience the type of love and joy that radiated from Toni.

"I wish you years of happiness, Cuz."

"Thank you." Toni leaned over and hugged Jada. "And thanks for all you did pulling the wedding and reception together. Everything turned out wonderful."

Jada shrugged. "My pleasure. Just be ready for my big day, whenever that might be." Jada returned her attention to the small group of men standing with Craig near the bar. "I guess it's true what they say. Beautiful people hang out together." All the men were as tall as Craig, at over six feet, and just as good looking in their black tuxedos sporting cummerbunds and bowties that matched the bridesmaid dresses.

"It looks that way doesn't it?"

Jada nodded and then turned to Toni. "Okay, answer this. What do I have to do to get a man as *fine* as yours, one who worships the ground I walk on, and is crazy wealthy?" She rolled her neck and slapped her hand down on the table. "I'm talkin' stinkin' rich as in lunch on the French Riviera and dinner at *La Vague d'Or* in Saint Tropez."

Toni shook her head, and a wide grin tilted the corners of her rose-colored lips. "I know suggesting that you lower your standards is out of the question. So I won't bother. I will say though, when the right man comes along, it's not going to matter if he's downright fine and stinkin' rich. All that's going to matter, or should matter is that he treats you right and loves you unconditionally."

"Uh, well, yeah, it *is* going to matter if he's fine and rich because if he isn't he won't be able to hang with me." Jada ignored the way Toni's perfectly arched eyebrows slanted in a frown. "Now what's the scoop on the hunks who just walked up to your new hubby? The one on the far right looks as if he could carry a small car on his back."

"Those are the guys he grew up with. Actually, today might be your lucky day." Toni perked up, a mischievous glint shined in her eyes as she adjusted the hem of her beaded lace wedding gown. "Craig's bringing Zack over."

"How does that make it my lucky day?"

"Because he's single and he's gawking at you."

Jada sized him up as he approached. At least six-one, broad shoulders that tapered down to a narrow waist, dark, spiked hair, and a powerful stride - he was a walking billboard for everything masculine. "Mmm, I don't think so. He's definitely a cutie in that Channing Tatum kind of way. But I like my men like I like my chocolate – dark and exceedingly rich."

"Is that right?" Toni placed her soda on the table and sat forward in her chair, her elbow on the table and amusement danced in her eyes. "Well, did I happen to mention that he's a professional football player who plays for the Cincinnati Cougars *and* has just renewed his contract for nine-point-five-million?"

Jada's mouth dropped open.

"Oh, and that's only for *one* year."

"*Damn!*" Jada smoothed down the front of her bridesmaid dress that stopped just above her knees and ran her fingers through her long auburn streaked curls. She quickly pulled a tube of lipstick from her strapless bra and ran the Coral Berry over her lips, and then took another glance at Craig's friend. "It's a good thing I'm switching over. I hear white chocolate, like milk, does a body good."

"What?" Toni narrowed her eyes. "I've never heard that before."

"Oh, hush up and tell me if I have any food in my teeth."

Toni shook her head and laughed. "Girl, you're a mess!"

"Hey, baby, are you feeling better?" Craig bent slightly and brushed Toni's bangs away from her forehead. "Did the soda help?" He extended his hand to help her rise to her feet and rubbed his large palm over her barely-there baby bump.

"Between the soda and the crackers you hunted down for me earlier, I'm feeling much better. You take such good care of me," Toni said in a baby-like voice.

"That's my job. I plan to spend the rest of my life taking very good care of you, Mrs. Logan." Craig lowered his head and his lips brushed against Toni's.

Jada rolled her eyes when the newlywed's lip-lock grew more intense and Toni's arms snaked around her husband's neck.

"You guys have a lifetime to play kissy-face." She stood and turned her gaze to the man standing next to her cousin-in-law. He was even sexier up close, and then he smiled. Her knees weakened. *Oh my God, he has dimples.* A sucker for a man with dimples, the once steady beat of her heart now pounded double-time. Her hand hovered over her chest as she struggled to fill her lungs with air. *Okay, just breathe.* She told herself over and over again.

"Are you all right?" the sexy gift from God asked, his palm at the small of her back sent a spark of desire shooting through her veins. "Can I get you something to drink?"

"Uh, no. No, I'm fine." She definitely had to pull herself together. Never has a man seen her sweat and she sure as hell wasn't going to let a cutie with a nine-point-five-million dollar contract see her off her game.

"Evidently we're invisible," Craig's friend said and removed his hand from her back. His voice intoxicatingly deep sent an exciting shiver up her spine. "I'm Zack Anderson."

Craig abruptly broke off the kiss with Toni. "Ah man, sorry you guys. Zack, this is Toni's cousin, JJ. I mean Jada Jenkins. JJ, this is one of my best friends, Zachary Anderson."

"Nice to meet you, Jada." Zack kissed the back of her hand and held on to the tips of her fingers while he stared into her eyes. "I've heard some nice things about you."

Jada swallowed hard and tried to throttle the dizzying current that raced through her body. *What the hell?* She had been in the midst of plenty of good-looking, wealthy men but never had one affected her like this. She eased her hand from his grasp and ran sweaty palms down the side of her dress as she regrouped, quickly plastering a flirtatious smile on her lips.

"Nice to meet you, Zachary."

"Please, call me Zack."

"Listen you two," Craig said from behind them, his arm around Toni. "My beautiful wife and I are going to greet our guest before the sendoff, and Zack," he leveled his friend with a pointed look, "behave yourself."

"I always do." Zack's piercing blue eyes roved and lazily appraised Jada, taking in all of her as if trying to memorize every intricate curve of her body.

5

Normally Jada would revolt against a man who openly gawked at her. Instead, she had the urge to stand perfectly still until he was done. *Damn, something is definitely wrong with me for enjoying the way he's sexing me up with his eyes.*

"Excuse me." Steven Jenkins, Jada's grandfather and the patriarch of the family jarred Jada out of her trance. He gave a quick nod to Zack before turning to her. "Your Highness, you're the only one of my granddaughters I haven't danced with yet. What do you say about cutting a rug with your old grandfather?"

"Oh, Grampa, there is nothing old about you and we don't say cutting a rug anymore. We just say dance." Jada grinned up at the man who had first given her the nickname Your Highness and the only man who had ever made her feel as if she were the most precious gift he'd ever received. Jada looped her arm through her grandfather's bent arm. "Stick with me. I'll keep you in the know."

He threw his head back and released a hearty laugh. "I don't know what I'm going to do with you."

Jada turned to Zack, still intrigued by the blue-eyed-dimpled god. "Grampa, I don't know if you've met Craig's friend Zack Anderson."

"Zack Anderson," Steven Jenkins repeated and extended his hand to Zack. "We haven't officially met, but of course, I know you're one of the league's top-scoring running backs. I'm a big fan. Nice to meet you, I'm Steven Jenkins."

"It's a pleasure, sir." Zack shook his hand. "Craig mentions you and your family often in conversation. I'm glad to meet you and the other members of your family," he said to Mr. Jenkins, but his potent gaze wandered to Jada.

"Well, a friend of Craig's is a friend of ours. Whenever the Cougars have a bye week, make sure you have Craig bring you to the house for Sunday brunch. We'd love to have you."

"I'd be honored." He bowed his head slightly and

diverted his attention back to Jada.

She ignored the giddiness fluttering inside her stomach. "It was nice meeting you," she said, still awed by the dimples that winked at her each time he flashed his million-dollar smile. "Hopefully we'll get a chance to chat before the reception ends." She cast a gracious smile and batted her eyes knowing the combination of the two always got her what she wanted. And she definitely wanted to get to know Zachery Anderson better.

"It looks as if you have another admirer," Jada's grandfather commented as they danced to John Legend's latest release. "He's a hell of a football player, and he seems like a nice young man."

Jada glanced over her grandfather's shoulder at Zack whose enticing gaze held hers captive. "Yes he does seem like a nice young man, doesn't he?"

***

Zack stared at Jada and her grandfather as they twirled around the dance floor in perfect sync. Intoxicating brown eyes that hinted of mischief and lips that were designed for kissing had left him mesmerized.

He first spotted her at the church and immediately found her captivating. At five-feet-five with full breasts, curvy hips, and long toned legs, most men in attendance couldn't take their gaze off of her. The gracefulness of her stroll down the aisle and the gentle sway of her hips in the fitted bridesmaid dress were hypnotic. Thankfully the Cougars were playing in town this weekend; otherwise he would have missed the wedding altogether. Craig had mentioned the Jenkins family, and the granddaughters who oversaw the day-to-day operations of Jenkins & Sons Construction, but he was going to have to talk to his long-time friend. The way Craig described the stunning Jenkins women hadn't done Jada justice.

Zack watched as the elder Jenkins moved his granddaughter smoothly across the dance floor as if dancing was something they did together all the time.

"She's way out of your league man. Besides, I can look at her and tell she's high maintenance and everyone knows how you feel about high maintenance women," Donny Caldron, a friend of Zack and Craig's from the old neighborhood said, and lifted his glass to his lips.

"Nah, I don't think she's high maintenance." Zack continued to observe her on the dance floor. He smiled to himself. She seemed to put a little extra hip action in her moves each time her grandfather released her hand. "She definitely has some sass, but I bet she's a real sweetheart once you get to know her, which I plan to do."

"Okay, so which one is she anyway? The carpenter? The electrician?"

"That's Jada. Can you believe she's a sheet metal worker?"

"Nope, but I can't believe any of them work construction. They make me want to tear down a house just so I can have them build it back up, brick by tantalizing brick."

Zack chuckled. While growing up, Donny was always the one who kept everyone laughing. With his laid-back attitude, many people would be surprised to know that he was the CEO for one of the city's largest pharmaceutical companies.

Zack shoved his hands into his pants pockets and rocked on the balls of his feet. "Well, I don't plan on tearing anything down. All I need is one date with her and she'll be mine."

Donny fell out laughing. "I think you've had one too many knocks upside the head out there on that football field because you're definitely talking crazy. That woman is not going out with your country ass," he joked. "Besides, I thought that since you're looking to retire next year you wanted to meet someone to settle down with. If that's still the case, you need to look elsewhere. She's not the one."

Donny always called him country despite the fact that they all grew up in Columbus, Ohio. "I'm no more country than you are and why do you think she's not the one for me? I beg to differ. Since she's a sheet metal worker, she clearly doesn't mind getting her hands dirty. I bet she's the outdoorsy type and enjoys hiking, biking and probably even fishing. Hell, she's exactly the type of woman I've been looking for - someone who's not too prissy to wear an old pair of jeans and a T-shirt, but someone who cleans up well and is classy enough to wow my family and friends."

Donny's brows drew together as he shook his head. "Apparently we're looking at two different women. I would bet my paycheck that the woman you just described is nowhere near the woman we're watching dance with the old dude. I don't care how many women have told you how *fine* you are or how many cater to your every desire once they find out how much you're worth. You don't stand a chance with her. She's too much woman for you."

"Whatever, dude." Zack nudged him in the shoulder. "Why don't we put a wager on whether or not she'll go out with me?" He removed a wad of money from his front pocket and started counting off bills.

"Man, you know I hate taking your money." Donny smirked. "But if you insist. I bet you a thousand bucks she turns your ass down cold."

"Yeah, we'll see about that."

***

"Grampa I'm impressed," Jada said. "You still have some moves. You're putting these young dudes to shame."

"Hey, I have to be able to keep up with all you kids." He spun her around and then pulled her back into his arms. "Your grandmother and I haven't seen you lately. What have you been up to?"

"Working. Grampa, I know you put Peyton in charge for a reason, but that girl has been working me like a slave." Her cousin Peyton Jenkins (PJ) was an electrician by trade and the senior construction manager for Jenkins & Sons Construction. "Do you know how many times I had to get my manicure touched up this week? Three times," Jada said without giving him a chance to respond. "I am so ready to find a wealthy husband, quit my job, and live happily-ever-after."

"Sweetheart, are you sure you're ready for marriage?"

She leaned away from her grandfather and frowned. "You know I am. I'm sick of working and don't get me started on taking out trash and making repairs around the house. I'm tired of doing everything for myself, and more importantly, I'm sick of the dating scene. I want to marry someone who is crazy in love with me and enjoys taking me out on the town. And Grampa, did you see this scar on my face?" She slowed her steps and pointed to the one-inch scratch under her jaw, near her chin. "I can't afford to get any more marks on my body from lugging sheet metal around all day."

Her grandfather hesitated and Jada groaned. She dropped her head on his shoulder, regretting all that she had shared, knowing she had just earned herself one of his famous lectures. Before she could retract her statement, he spoke.

"Your Highness, I know we have spoiled you and led you to believe that the world revolves around you, but let me explain something." He spun her around and then pulled her back into his arms. "It's not all about you. When some lucky young man finds *you*, and not the other way around, your main goal should be making sure that he's the man you want to spend the rest of your life with. Not the man who can buy you the latest Hermès Birkin handbag."

"I know Grampa," Jada responded, not surprised her grandfather knew anything about Hermès since it was one of her grandmother's favorite designers.

"Do you?" He slowed his steps and pulled back. His eyes narrowed and his gaze bored into her. "Because what I'm hearing from you is a lot of me, me, me, but sweetheart marriage takes work. Your parents and your grandmother and I might make marriage look easy, but we work hard to make our relationship work. Life, and marriage for that matter are not like Burger King. You can't always have it your way."

Jada shook her head and laughed. "I know Grampa. Don't worry I get what you're saying." She wrapped her arms around his neck and placed a kiss on his cheek. "When my Mr. Right comes along, I'll remember not to make everything all about me."

It was then she noticed Zack heading her way and her breath caught at his confident gait. *Mercy, this man personifies sexy.*

"Excuse me. May I cut in?"

CHAPTER TWO

Jada slowed as her grandfather glanced over his shoulder before he stopped completely. "I guess that depends on my granddaughter, young man." He returned his attention to Jada, and she gave a slight nod, her pulse inching up in speed. "She's all yours."

Zack reached for her hand and gently pulled her to him. Jada's heart beat double time. There was something about the ruggedly, handsome man that sent her senses out of control. When he wrapped his strong arm around her waist, and held her close, a lust-filled shudder gripped her body. *Good, Lord, he's all muscle.*

"I've been admiring you from across the room and couldn't let the evening pass without dancing with you."

He moved with such fluidity. Jada felt as if she were floating on a cloud, her feet barely touching the floor. She didn't know much about football, but she remembered her grandfather mentioning that Zack was a star running back. Apparently, his graceful moves served him well on the football field, as well as on the dance floor.

"I still can't get over you being a sheet metal worker. You definitely don't look like one." Zack pulled back slightly to look at her, and his piercing eyes made her miss a step. She loved dancing. Missing a step was unheard of. There was no way she was going to let the mere presence of a man rattle her.

She took a cleansing breath, pasted her most seductive smile on her lips, and glanced up at Zack. Her breath caught, and again her heart pounded uncontrollably when she met his gaze.

Oh, this is ridiculous. He's just a man, dammit.

Her usual self-talk wasn't working tonight, and she couldn't understand why. Sure he had the bluest eyes she'd ever stared into. Not that she had ever stared into the eyes of a blue-eyed hottie before, but his were mesmerizing. And it didn't help that the feel of his hard body rubbed up against hers had the throbbing pulse between her thighs beating a cadence she hadn't experienced in months. *Hell, it's no wonder I can't get myself together. The man is like an electric shock to the senses. Forget getting to know him. I need to get away from him.*

His grip tightened around her waist, preventing her planned retreat.

"So tell me about yourself. What do you do when you're not carrying duct work around?"

Jada blew out a breath. The anxiety consuming her was an unfamiliar feeling, her nerves raw and unprotected. Yet, on second thought, there was no way she would let nervousness get the best of her. It was time she poured on the old JJ charm.

"I stay busy." She loosened up, her fingers caressing the back of his neck and she put a little more hip motion in her moves as they slow danced to one of Alicia Keys' songs. "I play an intricate role in our family business, so that keeps me pretty busy. When I'm not working, or helping my mother and grandmother in their gardens, I do volunteer work around the city, helping those less fortunate." She shrugged, playing down her little white lies.

"That's cool. We have something in common. I like anything involving…."

Jada and Zack turned when loud laughter erupted from behind them, jarring them from their conversation.

Returning her gaze to Zack, Jada said, "I'm sure you've noticed that we have a large, close-knit family. They're a bit loud, overprotective at times and," she scrunched up her nose, "a little nosey."

His laugh rippled through the air. "I did notice. Uh, I mean I noticed how close everyone seems." Jada smiled at the way he tried to clean up his comment. "Considering how many families don't get along, it's nice to see that yours does. You and your cousins seem especially close."

Jada thought about Toni, Christina, Martina, and Peyton. She couldn't imagine her life without them. She and her cousins were closer than most sisters.

"Yeah, we're close. We hang out a lot. They often pull me into their shenanigans." She immediately thought back on the time when Craig caught her and Toni hiding a drunk man in her grandparent's bathroom. Jada smiled at the memory.

When she glanced up, Zack flashed her a smile and a warm sensation embraced her like a fox fur coat on a cold winter's night. She lowered her eyes to keep from being caught up in those dimples of his that kept making an appearance and screwing with her senses.

"Do you have any siblings?" Zack dipped her. A tiny chirp of surprise flew through her lips before he pulled her back into his arms.

Okay, now he's just showing off. But she had to admit, she liked a man who could talk, dance, and dip a woman without missing a beat. Her mind wandered to a naked Zack, hovering above her in bed. Would he bring the same confidence and suaveness to her bedroom? Could he kiss and make her body hum the way… *Wait!* She shook her head slightly. *Now where did that come from?*

"Jada?"

Her eyes shot up. "Oh, I'm sorry. What did you say?"

"Do you have any siblings?"

"Oh, yeah, I … um have two older brothers. What about you? Any siblings? Kids? Uh … a wife, ex-wives?" Remembering her ultimate goal of marrying rich, and quitting her job, she started her mission of getting to know Mr. Potential.

He smiled. "I have two brothers also, one younger and one older. And I have an older sister. I don't have any children, but I would love to have enough to make at least a basketball team of my own." He winked. "Oh and I don't have an ex-wife *or* a wife, but I'm looking." He spun her and pulled her back into his arms, his mouth only inches from hers. "Any more questions?"

Jada stared at his lips. A brazen warmth attacked her body. The desire to kiss him so strong it took everything she had not to reach up and pull his face closer.

"Uh, what do you do for fun?" she finally asked, forcing herself not to act on the lustful thoughts running rampant through her mind.

"I love the outdoors. Camping, snowboarding, zip lining, sports – especially football. All of it. If it's an outdoor adventure, I'm all in. I also enjoy anything where I can use my hands." His voice dropped an octave, and he pulled her closer. It wasn't hard for Jada to figure out he was talking about more than just outdoor activities.

"I see."

"How do you feel about those types of activities?" He glanced down at her.

"I'm pretty much a go with the flow kinda girl." She lied. She hated the outdoors, especially if it meant she'd get dirty or sweaty.

"Heeeeyyy."

Jada startled, hearing her cousin Toni sing out when the DJ played the next song. Justin Timberlake's voice pumped through the speakers and by the sound of the crowd, the song was a favorite.

Jada glanced to her right in time to see Toni rush Craig out onto the dance floor. She hoped Toni's new husband knew what he was getting into. A huge Justin Timberlake fan, Toni always sang along with him – as loud as she could. Too bad she couldn't carry a tune if it were packed in a bag and strapped to her back.

Zack sang along to Timberlake's "Not A Bad Thing," his baritone voice caressing Jada's ear, sending sparks of desire to every nerve ending in her body.

Ah, hell, and he can sing? Jada shivered. *That's it. I have to get away from this man. I need to regroup.*

Zack slowed and loosened his grip, but didn't let go. "Maybe you and I can go out sometime." A slight smile graced his tempting lips.

"Uhh…"

"Excuse me." Christina's voice came out of nowhere and Jada's body flooded with relief from the interruption. Her cousin stood next to them. "I'm so sorry to intrude, but Jada, duty calls. Peyton needs our help."

"Oh, okay." Jada could kiss her cousin. Normally Christina's timing was awful, but right now, Jada couldn't get away from Zack fast enough. He unsettled her in ways she couldn't explain.

She glanced at her handsome dance partner and pulled away. "I'm sorry. A bridesmaid work is never done. Thanks for the dance." She grabbed Christina's arm and hurried away from the dance floor.

***

What just happened?

Zack stood in the middle of the dance floor, staring after Jada. Had he moved too fast? She ran from him as if he had threatened her life.

Damn. Maybe I shouldn't have asked her out yet.

He rubbed his forehead, turning to leave the dance floor.

Everything about the woman was perfect. A construction worker who loved the outdoors, a volunteer worker, family oriented, and she was one of the most beautiful women he'd ever met. If that weren't enough, she fit perfectly in his arms, like a missing puzzle piece, created especially for him. And damn if the exquisite scent of her perfume didn't have him wanting to chase after her.

When Zack glanced up, Donny still stood where he had left him earlier. If the grin on his face was any indication, Zack knew his friend had witnessed Jada running off.

Zack cursed under his breath again. The last thing he needed was for Donny to start giving him a hard time about chasing a woman away.

"So wh—"

"Don't say anything," Zack said when he approached his friend. Donny handed him a beer bottle. "We didn't get a chance to discuss going out before she was pulled away by her cousin."

"Uh huh. It looked more like she was running away, which doesn't surprise me. You probably bored her to death."

"Whatever, man. I assure you, within the next two weeks, I will have a date with the beautiful Jada JJ Jenkins."

"Yeah, we'll see. Did you even get her digits?"

"Don't need them." Zack glanced in the direction that she'd disappeared. "I'll find her."

Donny shook his head. "I still think you're getting in over your head man. She is out of your league. I know women like her."

"What do you mean like her? Gorgeous? Construction worker? Black? What?" Zack got in his face, struggling to keep his anger at bay. "You think just because your skin is a closer shade of color to hers than mine that you know all about her?" Donny narrowed his eyes and took a step back. "Oh, so what, now you don't have anything to say?"

"You know what? You're trippin'," Donny sipped the

amber-colored liquor in his glass. "I'm going to give you a pass since I can tell you're feelin' this girl. But don't you ever," he pointed his finger in Zack's face, "step to me like that again. I'm tryin' to help your ass and you gon' trip like this? Zack, man, a few months ago you almost lost everything to that gold-diggin' heifer, Leslie. You're my boy. Do you think I want to see you go through that shit again? This Jenkins woman might not be like your ex, but I'm telling you man, she's not what you think. She *is* high maintenance and probably everything else you said you didn't want in a woman. You're just not trying to see it."

Zack set his beer bottle on a nearby table and shoved his hands into the front pockets of his pants. He and Donny grew up together. Zack knew he had his best interest in mind, and he also knew that Jada wasn't anything like Leslie — his gold-digging ex-fiancée.

***

Jada held on tight to Christina's arm and pulled her into the bridesmaid's room. "You care to tell me what that was all about?" Christina asked rubbing her arm. "I have never seen you behave so egregious toward a man before, especially a pulchritudinous-looking man."

Jada rolled her eyes at her cousin's constant use of words that no one knew the meaning of. She moved across the room and stopped to primp in front of a full-length mirror. "I didn't behave egregaga … or whatever the heck you said." She ran her fingers through her long curls and smoothed out her dress before turning to her cousin. "I walked away because you said Peyton needed us."

"Then why'd you drag me in here? We're supposed to be in Toni's room," she glanced at her watch, "in five minutes."

Jada stared at her cousin wondering how much to tell her. Christina Jenkins, also known as CJ, was one of her best friends as well as her landlord. Jada had moved in with her a year ago, planning to stay only a few months until she saved enough money to buy a condominium. However, compulsive shopping prevented her from saving enough to get the place she'd been admiring in Hyde Park.

"I think I'm losing my edge with men." Jada dropped into a striped upholstered chair near a bookshelf. "This guy Zack is a friend of Craig's and there is something about him that unnerves me."

Concern marred Christina's face, and she pulled a nearby chair close to Jada. "What?" She brushed her out-of-control curls away from her face. "I can't believe that any of Craig's friends would be a jerk. He doesn't—"

"Oh, no, no, no. He doesn't unnerve me in a negative way. It's more like just looking at him makes me sweat. And you know I don't like to sweat. My heart rate kicks up, and my words get all jumbled, and when he's close to me, I feel as if I'm hyperventilating.

Christina sat back and folded her arms, a small smile tilting the corners of her lips. "Well, I'll be. I can't believe Your Highness is affected by a man." She giggled. "I'll admit he's attractive, but you've gone out with plenty of gorgeous men. So what is it about this guy? Is it because he's white?"

She shook her head. "No, his race doesn't matter." The affect Zack had on her internally is what warranted concern. There was only one other man who had ever made her stomach churn in the way she had experienced tonight. *Dion Greely*. The only man she had ever loved and the only man who had ever ripped out her heart and crushed it into tiny, little pieces.

Her thoughts skittered back to Zack. He might not be another Dion, but she couldn't ignore how being in his presence shook her to the core. Those twin dimples … those eyes. His list of attributes were so long she didn't know if it was just one thing that made her a bumbling fool whenever he was near her.

"By the gleam in your eyes, I'd say that this is a case of indubitable attraction. Yet, it has to be more than that to have you in here hiding out."

"I know. There's something about this man. I don't know much about him, but already I know he's different than the type of men I usually date. He's genuine, confident without being arrogant and humble without coming off like a chump. He's a great listener, and he's not ruled by money or what he has." And that's what scared her. Arrogance and self-centeredness, she could handle. Sweet, kind, and the fall-in-love-easily type, she couldn't handle.

"Hold up. I know you're good, but are you telling me you figured all of that out with only one dance?"

Before Jada could respond, the door flew open. Martina Jenkins, MJ, stood in the entryway with her arms braced against the doorjamb and a scowl on her perfectly made up face. She had already been in a bad mood. Having to wear such a *frilly* dress with *too-tall* sandals didn't help. Now the murderous glare she shot Jada and Christina would have made others take cover, but they were used to their cousin's theatrics.

"Do you know how long I've been looking for you guys? What part of meet in Toni's room at seven-thirty didn't you two understand?"

"Ah, don't get your grandma panties in a bunch. We're coming," Jada said.

They both stood and followed MJ out of the room. Jada turned to Christina and whispered. "I trust that our conversation stays between us."

"Of course, but I want to explore your problem a little more when we get home," she joked, sounding like a therapist.

Jada smiled and shook her head. As far as she was concern, there was no problem. As long as she stayed away from Zack Anderson.

CHAPTER THREE

"You might as well pay up, dude. You owe me a thousand bucks." Donny grabbed another slice of pizza and sat back in the leather, theater room seat to watch Monday night football. "It's been almost two weeks and Jada Jenkins hasn't given you the time of day. Pay up. Pay up now!"

"Man, please. I ain't payin' nothin'. I still have four days to convince her to go out with me." Zack took a swig of Gatorade. "And I can't believe you're trying to get me to pay before the bet has officially ended."

After receiving Jada's telephone number from Craig, Zack had called her three times since the wedding reception, but she had yet to return any of his calls. Now hindsight, Zack wondered if maybe she would've been more receptive of his calls had he asked for her number directly.

"I can't believe you're interested in this woman. Especially when you've shot down advances from others. Personally, I think you should give Monica a chance. She's *fine* as hell and a real sweetheart."

"I don't trust her."

Donny shook his head and laughed. "Man you don't trust anyone. You act as if all women are out to take advantage of you." Zack turned to Donny with a raised eyebrow. "Okay, I can see why you'd be a little leery considering your last two relationships. I'm still trippin' that Leslie accused you of domestic abuse. Yet, at some point, you're going to have to give someone a chance."

"That's why I'm trying to hook up with Jada."

"I just don't understand that." Donny wiped his mouth and sat back in his seat, studying Zack. "That honey, has gold-digger tattooed on her beautiful forehead. I saw her in the lobby taking a picture when I left the reception. Peeking over her shoulder, hand on her hip, her leg flipped up with the heel of her expensive shoes touching that sweet round ass."

"Hey, watch yourself!" A smoldering flame of desire crept through Zack just listening to Donny's assessment of Jada, but he couldn't sit there listening to his friend talk about her sweet ass.

Donny held up his hands in mock surrender. "No disrespect, dude, I'm just sayin'." He shrugged. "Seriously though, a construction worker salary didn't pay for those high-priced shoes or that Rolex she was wearing. "

His friend might've been right, but Zack couldn't ignore how the air around him seemed electrified when she was near. He'd been with his share of women, but none affected him the way she had.

"Maybe Jada ignoring your calls is a sign for you to move on. The last thing you need is more BS from another tryflin', money-hungry woman."

"I'm not giving up just yet." Zack ran his hand over his mouth and stopped at his chin, rubbing the scruff growing from not shaving in a couple of days. "I think I'm going to try a different approach with Ms. Jada Jenkins. Apparently I need to do something to get her atten—"

"Are you expecting someone else?" Donny interrupted. "I think I just heard your doorbell."

"Nope." Zack picked up the remote and turned down the

volume of the home theater system. The doorbell rang again. "I'll be back in a sec." He stood and headed toward the stairs.

Walking through his large kitchen, Zack glanced at the home's alarm keypad located in the short hall that led to the attached garage. He hadn't set the system to close the front gate automatically once Donny entered onto the property. Pushing a couple of buttons, he made sure the gate closed automatically going forward.

He opened the door and stared at the person standing on the other side of the threshold, shocked to see her on his doorstep. His gaze traveled the length of the statuesque body from her thick, long tresses flowing over bare shoulders, to a perfectly made up face on down to the purple dress with the sheer side panels that hugged every curve like a second skin.

"Now that you have thoroughly checked me out, aren't you going to invite me in?"

Her syrupy voice snapped him to attention and anger clawed its way from his gut to his throat, threatening to burst free.

"Hell nah I'm not inviting you in! You're not even supposed to be on my property. Why are you here, Leslie?"

"I need to talk to you and you haven't returned any of my calls."

"Are you serious?" he asked, shocked to see her standing there. "We don't have anything to discuss. So you can just go and crawl back—"

"Baby, please. I know you hate me, but you have to let me explain."

"Explain?" Zack gripped the doorframe, rage for what she had put him through pulsed through his veins. "What's there to explain? You lied about being pregnant, and I agreed to marry you. Then you lied about having a miscarriage and who knows what else you lied about while we were together. And if that wasn't enough, your ass went to the cops, claiming that I beat you!"

"But Zack—"

"But Zack nothing!" He growled and slowly approached her, but stopped. "Donny, get up here!" He would never put his hands on a woman with evil intentions, but she had accused him of doing just that once, and he wanted to make sure a witness was nearby just in case she tried it again.

Donny bounded up the stairs. "I'm right behind you," his friend said. Zack knew when Donny saw who was at the door, he would understand.

"Was that really necessary?" Leslie huffed.

Pointing his finger at her, Zack inched closer, remembering all that she had put him through including how she forged his name on one of his checks.

"Your lying, scheming ass should be in jail somewhere. You almost cost me my career, and you have the nerve to ring my doorbell?" He took two steps back. Taking a deep breath and releasing it slowly, he returned his attention to the woman he once thought he loved. "There was nothing I wouldn't have done for you and you know it. Yet, you tried to ruin me. I'm done with you."

"I'm not giving up until you hear me out."

He held up his hand. "You know what…" He didn't bother finishing the sentence. Talking to her was like banging his head against a brick wall. He stepped back into the house without giving her a second glance. "You have twenty seconds to get off my property or I'm calling the cops." He slammed the door in her face.

I wasted a year of my life with her.
***

"Nick, I need you and Jada to start on the Henderson-Clark project downtown," Peyton Jenkins said standing at the front of the conference room near the massive size white board. "And Jada, before you start complaining, it's a dirty job, but somebody has to do it."

Jada's mouth dropped open. "I didn't even say anything. It's mid-week, and I haven't complained … to you all week."

PJ turned to write on the board. "I figured you were due for a complaint." Everyone in the room chuckled, mainly her family members. Jada didn't appreciate being singled out. Sure, she complained sometimes, but who wouldn't? Lately, most of their jobs were in the nastiest furnace rooms or on the roof of the tallest buildings in Cincinnati. She wasn't afraid of heights, but she didn't look forward to hanging off the side of the roof of a thirty-story office building installing wall flashing.

"In Jada's defense," her cousin Nick started, "I have to admit that this week she's been on her best behavior and hasn't complained once."

Jada wanted to stick out her tongue at PJ, but thought it might be a little too childish. At twenty-four, Jada was working hard to get her family to see her as a mature woman and not the baby of the family who used to get most of them in trouble. Her oldest cousin, Nick, always looked out for her, giving her the least amount of grief. Unlike his twin brother, Nate, who lived to taunt her.

"If Jada hasn't complained, she must be sick. I can't recall a day she hasn't griped about a broken nail, a scar, or her stupid hair," Martina chimed in, sitting across from Jada, a wicked grin spread across her face. "So, are you sick or something?"

Jada narrowed her eyes at her cousin, who was always trying to start something. "MJ, you aren't going to always have me around to pick on."

"Maybe not, but in the meantime –"

"Can we get back to business?" Peyton placed a hand on her hip. She gave both Jada and Martina a look that halted all conversation.

Jada half listened while Peyton made assignments. Others in the room shared progress reports and material shortage updates. Jada loved her family and the family business more than anything, but she was ready for something different in her life.

"Does that work for you, JJ?"

Jada's gaze shot to Peyton, not having a clue as to what she was about to agree to.

"That's fine," she mumbled, knowing PJ would bust her out if she knew she wasn't paying attention. Jada looked over at Nick who grinned and gave her thumbs up.

Oh great. I'll probably be crawling through ductwork today.

Thirty minutes later, the meeting ended. It was only eight o'clock in the morning and Jada felt as if she had already put in a full day of work. She hadn't been sleeping well thanks to her nightly dreams of Zack Anderson. For the life of her, she couldn't figure out what about the man turned her mind to mush and her body into a fiery furnace every time she thought of him. That one dance had left her aroused and aching to be touched by him again.

"JJ, I'll meet you at the van in ten minutes." Nick broke into her thoughts on his way out the door.

"Sounds good." She headed downstairs to the reception area. She needed a strong cup of coffee. The coffee in the lobby was always more potent than the coffee Peyton made before the staff meetings.

"Oh, JJ, I'm glad you're still here. You just had a delivery," the receptionist, Tammy, said.

Jada poured the dark, hot liquid into a Styrofoam cup while Tammy stood and walked to the hall closet. Jada's eyes lit up, and a bout of giddiness raced through her veins at the sight of a huge white box.

"What is it?" She walked around the desk. The only things she'd ordered recently were two pairs of Kate Spade sandals and a handbag, but those items had arrived days earlier. She assumed the contents had to be a gift from one of her admirers.

"I don't know. A courier service delivered the package about ten or fifteen minutes ago."

Jada skimmed the box, and the only writing on it was her name across the top.

Tammy handed her a box cutter and Jada eagerly cut through the tape, hoping it was a gift from Marcus Hightower, the president of a bank. They'd been out a number of times and lately, he'd been sending gifts on a regular basis.

Excitement raced through her body as she cut away the tape. She loved surprises almost as much as she loved gifts.

At that moment, Martina and Christina came down the stairs discussing a project.

"So what's all of this?" MJ stopped next to Jada. CJ stood on Jada's left. "Another gift from one of your boy-toys?"

"Oh, don't hate. I can't help it if I have generous admirers." Jada opened the box and yanked out all of the newspaper surrounding two smaller boxes. More excitement bubbled within her as she tore through the first of the two smaller boxes.

Her hands stilled, and the smile dropped from her lips when she lifted the item from the box.

"What the hell is that?" MJ asked, disgust dripping from her words. "Tell me someone didn't send you a purple power drill."

"Well, that's what it looks like." CJ grinned as Jada frowned at the unusual gift. "It might seem like a fatuous type of gift, but personally, I think it shows signs of the sender's solicitous nature."

Both Jada and Martina turned to Christina. Jada narrowed her eyes. "What the heck does fatuous mean?" CJ's word-a-day mission to improve her vocabulary was driving everyone crazy. Jada lifted her hands and shook her head. "No, no don't tell me. I don't care."

"What you should be caring about is what type of knucklehead sends a sheet metal worker a *purple* drill? It should be against the law for a company to even make crap like this. You drop it once, and I guarantee this junk will crumble into a thousand pieces." MJ took it upon herself to pull out the next box and ripped the package open as if Jada wasn't standing there. Then she burst out laughing. "*And* purple tools? This is too much!" She laughed harder, pounding the counter in an effort to catch her breath.

"Who sent all of this?" CJ stretched her neck to peer into the box. "Someone trying to expiate for an atrocity they perpetrated against you? I have to say, these accoutrements are going to look cute on your tool belt."

MJ whirled on her. "Stop it! Who the hell uses *expiate* or *accoutrements* in a simple conversation?"

"Hey! Don't get mad at me if I use words that are arcane by people who only pick up a book sporadically."

"Well, use another one of those stupid words while we're standing here and I'm going to use a few choice words...."

Jada tuned out her cousins. Curious by the gifts, she searched through the box for a note. She found a small, white envelope and quickly pulled out a card.

Beautiful tools for a beautiful woman. You left the reception before I had a chance to ask you out officially. Have dinner with me this Saturday night. Zack.

Jada shook her head. First, the telephone calls from him that she had ignored, and then the nightly dreams. Now gifts. She reread the card that included his telephone number and shoved it back into its envelope. She appreciated the gesture, but her family and coworkers would laugh her right off the job if they caught her using purple tools. The teasing was bad enough with her arriving to work in full makeup, perfect hair and polished nails. There was no way she was giving them more ammunition to use against her. Besides, she couldn't go out with Zack.

Martina grabbed hold of Jada's wrist and yanked the small envelope out of her hand. She read the card. "Whoever this Zack person is, you need to school him on what type of tools real construction workers use." She lifted the purple drill and held the power tool up, turning the base from side to side. "I wish you would show up on a site with this thing. You think you get picked on now, you wouldn't last a day with this crap."

Jada didn't bother mentioning to Martina that she was the main person who gave her a hard time about any and everything.

"Don't you have something to do?" Jada asked MJ, snatching the card from her and stuffing it back into the envelope.

Martina laughed and shoved the drill back into the box. "Don't get mad at me if *Zack* doesn't know the difference between toy drills and real drills. Who is this Zack person anyway? One of your new lackeys?"

"Zack Anderson," Christina blurted out.

Martina's smile slipped from her lips. "Zack Anderson? *The* Zack Anderson – the world's greatest running back who plays for Cincinnati? The guy who can carry two defensive ends on his back and still make a first down? Last year's MVP? *That* Zack Anderson?"

"The one and only." Christina grinned but pinched her lips together when Jada narrowed her eyes. Jada didn't want MJ making a big deal about her acquaintance with Zack since she had no intention of going out with him.

"Hold up. So you're dating Zack Anderson." Martina grinned and rubbed her hands together. "Finally! You've hooked up with someone worthy to date a Jenkins girl. I need you to see if he can get me some tickets to this Sunday's game against Pittsburgh. It's been sold out for weeks."

"We're not dating." Jada shoved everything back into the box. "You're on your own, getting tickets. Tammy," Jada slid the box across the counter, "can you contact the courier who delivered this and have them pick it up?"

Tammy arched an eyebrow. "Are you sure?"

"Positive."

"Why are you sending this stuff back?" Martina grabbed

hold of the box before Tammy could walk away with it. "At least call the guy. Or better yet, I can call him and thank him for you."

"You were the one going on and on about purple tools. Why should I thank him or keep them?"

"Jada, you of all people can't be this stupid. Especially since you tend to only date guys with a six-figure income. Do you have any idea who you're dealing with? Clearly, you don't know what he's worth. Otherwise, you would be falling all over yourself to call him.

"You act as if money is my only motivation. Yes I want to live a comfortable life, but it's about more than money."

"Yeah, tell it to someone who doesn't know you."

"Whatever. You should try minding your own business for a change." Jada turned to Tammy. "Please send it back. If there's a fee, let me know, and I'll take care of the cost."

Jada walked away from the reception area and headed to the parking lot, ignoring anything more that Martina had to say. MJ didn't understand. There was no way Jada was going out with someone who unnerved her the way Zack did. For the first time in her life, she didn't care how much he was worth.

CHAPTER FOUR

"Good practice today guys," the Cincinnati Cougars coach said to the players as they exited the locker room.

Zack grabbed his duffle bag and slung it over his shoulder, pulling his cell phone out of the side pocket. He entered his security code to listen to his voicemail. Five messages and not one of them was the call he had hoped to receive – the call from Jada. She still hadn't responded to any of his voice messages, but he thought for sure he would've heard from her by now, especially after the gift he had sent to her the day before.

"Later Zack," someone called out. Turning he spotted Ted and Randy, the quarterback and a wide receiver twenty feet behind him.

He threw up his hand and waved. "You guys have a good one." Slipping on his shades, he approached his Mercedes CL600, a gift to himself for obtaining career-high rushing yards last season. Tossing his bag in the trunk, he climbed in and headed home.

Zack's mind immediately went to thoughts of Jada, unable to stop thinking about her. Women normally threw themselves at him, but not her. She didn't seem to care that they had a connection. He felt it, and based on the desire he saw in her big, bright eyes when they danced, she felt it too. Now all he had to do was convince her to go out with him.

Thirty minutes later, Zack pulled into his three-car garage, closing the overhead door behind him. He sat in the well-lit space and glanced around. When he had purchased the five bedroom, five and a half bathroom, Indian Hill home in Cincinnati eight years earlier, it was with plans of filling it with a wife and children. Instead, he had filled his life with material things. A Land Rover took up one of the stalls and a Harley-Davidson CVO Ultra Classic he never drove due to a stipulation in his football contract, took up the last stall. He had everything a man could want, but not what he really desired – a family. He loved all the space and the privacy the home provided, but lately it was starting to feel too quiet.

He climbed out of the car and strolled into the house. His stomach growled the moment he entered. The smell of onions and a hint of bacon teased his senses. Stepping into his home wasn't so bad when he knew his housekeeper was there. Mrs. Mallard only came three days a week during the football season since he spent much of his time away. Zack didn't know what she'd prepared for dinner, but it was guaranteed to be good.

He dropped his bag on the floor next to the counter that held a large white box and a note from his housekeeper.

Hi Zack, I'm not sure if you remembered that I had to leave early for an appointment today. Your dinner is in the oven and a special dessert for you is in the refrigerator. Oh, and this box was delivered shortly after you left this morning. Have a good night, and I'll see you in the morning. Mrs. Mal.

Zack skimmed the writing on top of the box and paused when he noticed Jada's name.

What the heck?

The company he had purchased the tools from was supposed to deliver the box to her, not him. Opening the box, he immediately noticed a pink sticky note attached to the card he had sent with the gift.

Thanks for the equipment, but purple tools are never a good idea to send to a construction worker. But if you really want to do something for me, how about two tickets to this Sunday's game? JJ

Zack braced his hands on top of the counter. He hadn't pegged Jada as a football fan, especially since she hadn't asked him anything about football like most people did. He scanned the note again. She hadn't said anything about going out with him, but she hadn't said no either.

A smile spread across Zack's mouth as an idea formed. He pulled his cell phone from the pocket of his jeans. *Maybe I'll pay Jada a visit before practice tomorrow.* If she wanted tickets to the game, then tickets were what she'd get.

***

"I need to find her a man," Jada said when she and Nick stepped out of Peyton's office. "She's been harassing us about this job all week. Clearly, she needs a distraction." The project they were working on had one setback after another, and her cousin acted as if they were goofing off or something.

"Peyton was right." Nick stopped, in the middle of the hallway, to tie his boots. "That job should've been completed by now. Today we're knocking it out. No excuses."

"Okay, but is it too late to get a cherry picker out there? I'm still not feeling the idea of working on that rickety scaffolding, especially since it's so windy today."

"I thought you said the cherry picker felt too unsteady."

The cherry picking machine they often used on outside work had a long metal arm that could extend several floors and a small basket on the end that barely accommodate two people. It did make Jada nervous. Yet, the scaffolding they were using freaked her out more.

They strolled past a couple of offices and walked toward

the front stairs. Jada wondered about the silence. Rarely was it that quiet on the second-floor first thing in the morning.

"The cherry picker makes me a little nervous, but lately it doesn't seem as scary as the…" Jada's voice trailed off when she saw at least ten of her family members huddled at the front desk.

"Well, I'll be damn. Zack Anderson," Nick mumbled and hurried down the rest of the stairs.

Jada's heart did somersaults inside her chest. He had his head down signing autographs and laughing with her family and other staff members. She couldn't get her legs to move. The man was gorgeous in a tuxedo, but wearing a baseball cap, a fitted T-shirt that stretched across his wide chest, and jeans that hung low on his hips, he looked downright sinful.

As if sensing her gaze on him, he glanced toward the stairs, and their eyes met, sending her pulse into overdrive. *Good Lord this man is gorgeous. Got my dang mouth watering. But why is he here?* Somehow, he had managed to get her telephone number, and she thought he would have caught a hint that she wasn't interested when she didn't return his calls. Now this.

"Jada," Martina said in a sing-song voice. "You have a visitor."

Jada finally forced herself forward, not missing the curious stares. She walked right up to Zack and whispered near his ear, "What are you doing here?" Deeply inhaling, his familiar fragrance gripped her, making her want to wrap her arms around his neck and breathe in again. She had to keep herself from moaning and quickly stepped back.

"I got your note."

Jada narrowed her eyes at him. "What note?"

"Yes!" Martina whooped, pumped her fist in the air, and then did a little dance. "I'm going to the game. I'm going to the game."

"Hold up. What did you do?" Jada ground out as she approached her cousin.

"Alright, that's my cue," someone said and others agreed while saying their goodbyes to Zack.

Plenty of times, Jada wanted to strangle MJ, but with this little stunt, someone was going to have to pull her off of her cousin.

"I figured the least you could do was thank him for the tools, even if you didn't want them."

"And." Christina walked up next to Jada. "What else did you do?"

"Oh, so what, y'all tryin' to gang up on me?" MJ folded her arms across her chest, her signature smirk planted on her face. "You do remember the last time you two tried to come at me don't you?"

Jada blew out a breath and then turned back to Zack. "I'm sorry for whatever she did. That was nice of you to send the tools, but—"

"But you don't do purple tools, right?"

Jada smiled and shook her head. She could only imagine what MJ had put in her note. "No. I don't, but it was very sweet of you."

He lifted what appeared to be two tickets in his hand. "So I take it you really don't want these?"

"I … uh…"

"Oh, those are mine!" MJ practically knocked Jada over to get to Zack, who lifted the tickets out of her reach. "I'll admit that I'm the one who wrote the note about the tickets, and I signed her name, but it was for a good reason." Her cousin's words flew out of her mouth as fast as a speeding bullet.

"Oh, this ought to be good," Zack chuckled, an amused expression on his face.

"Well, it's like this, Zack." MJ leaned against the front counter. "Can I call you Zack?"

Jada rolled her eyes at her cousin, but Zack laughed and nodded.

"Well Zack, she wants to go out with you, but she's

taking a break from dating."

What the heck is she talking about? Jada fumed, her hands planted on her hips. This time MJ had gone too far.

"Is that right?" He looked Jada up and down, the lustful perusal reminding her of the way he had checked her out at the reception. "Well, how about this." He returned his attention to MJ. "If you get your cousin to go out with me tomorrow, these third row seats, behind Cincinnati's bench on the 50-yard-line tickets, are yours." He held them up.

MJ's mouth dropped open, and Jada couldn't remember a time when she'd seen her cousin speechless. Of course, the silence was short-lived.

"Jada," Martina said, her tone low and lethal, "your ass is going out with him if I have to tie you to the passenger seat of his car. I want those tickets."

"Uhh, excuse me," Peyton stood in the middle of the stairwell gripping a clipboard. "Unless you all want to be looking for another job come Monday morning, I suggest you get out of here and get to work."

"I'm outta here." CJ darted for the back door that lead to the service vans in the parking lot.

"I have to take care of one thing," MJ said, "and then I'll head out. But first, I need to talk to Jada." MJ grabbed Jada by the arm. "Zack, we'll be right back. Don't go anywhere." MJ pulled Jada into the small conference room to the left of the receptionist area.

"I'm going to kill you! I'm not going out with him," Jada said the moment her cousin closed the door. "So you might as well say goodbye to those tickets."

"What's up with you? The guy is *fine*, stinkin' rich, and comes across like a man who is willing to worship the ground you walk on. So what's the problem? He meets your criteria."

Jada walked over to the large window, staring out at nothing in particular. Part of her wanted to go out with Zack, but she didn't like not being in control. He made her nervous. Something that rarely happened, especially around men.

"I know it can't be because he's white," Martina interrupted her thoughts, "because you've never discriminated against any man, especially if he has money."

"It has nothing to do with him being Irish, Italian, or whatever his ethnic makeup is. I just don't want to go out with him." Jada turned to face her cousin.

"I think you do." MJ leaned against the wall and glanced at her watch. "You just don't want me to get those tickets."

"Girl, this ain't got nothing to do with you. How would you feel if I told Senator Paul Kendricks that you were interested in dating him and then lured him here?"

If looks could kill, Jada would have shriveled up and crumbled to the ground. Everyone knew Martina Jenkins would rather chew nails than even hear the name Paul Kendricks. Her cousin had never even met the man, yet she hated his guts. Active with the carpenters union in Cincinnati, Martina looked at anyone who opposed unions, as the enemy. Paul Kendricks was definitely the enemy.

"Why'd you have to bring his name up?" Martina eased up to Jada. "And how can you compare *Zack* Anderson to that man? Do you know anything about that guy standing out there wanting to go out with you? Do you know how much money he contributes to charities every year, or how many hours he volunteers at homeless shelters and food banks?"

Jada sighed. She didn't know anything about Zack except for what he'd told her while they were dancing.

"Listen. Zack might be one of the nicest people in the world, but is it such a bad thing that I'm not interested in going out with him?" Her reasons for not wanting to be near him suddenly seemed wimpy, especially since she was seriously attracted to him. She liked to be in control and Zack seemed to zap some of that power she was accustomed to wielding.

"Jada, I know I give you a hard time sometimes."

Jada leaned back and narrowed her eyes at her cousin. "*Sometimes?* Try all the time."

Since they were kids, Martina picked on her for one reason or another. Though Jada had to admit, when it came to looking out for the family, MJ was probably the most loyal and would do anything for a Jenkins. She was the type of person who felt it was okay to bully her family, but let someone else mess with them, and she was ready to fight.

"Okay, you're right." MJ conceded. "But just this once can you do this for me? I'm not going to promise that I'll leave you alone going forward because I'd be lying." Jada had to chuckle at that. "But I need you to consider going out with Zack. I will probably never in this lifetime be able to afford those type of football tickets that he's offering. Please … just do it for me."

It's not always about you Your Highness. Her grandfather's words came to mind. All of her life her motto had been – *it's all about me.* For the most part, that motto had gotten her everything she wanted.

"Besides, I've never known you to turn down dinner at a fancy restaurant or an evening out rubbing shoulders with the rich and famous."

The door opened, and Nick stuck his head in. "Any day now, JJ. If you're not outside in five minutes, you'll have to get to the site the best way you can." He closed the door without giving her a chance to respond.

She sighed, rolled her eyes, and her shoulders slumped before she looked back at her cousin. "All right, I'll go out with him just so that you can get the tickets. But you owe me. You owe me big!" Martina wrapped Jada in a bear hug as they made their way to the door.

"Okay, I'll go out with you," Jada said to Zack when she and Martina walked back into the reception area. Jada grabbed a business card from the counter and jotted her number on the back. "That's for just in case you don't still have my number. Give me a call tonight, and we can make arrangements."

His lips tilted into a small smile, and he handed the tickets to Martina, but didn't take his gaze from Jada.

"Thank you! Good luck on Sunday. I hope the team wins," MJ said before she grabbed her tool bucket from next to the counter and hurried off toward the back of the building.

Zack lifted Jada's hand. "I'm not sure what your cousin said to convince you, but I guarantee you won't be sorry." He kissed the back of her hand. An electric charge shot up her arm and liquid heat spread through her body.

Jada swallowed hard as she stared into his crystal blue eyes. *God give me strength.*

CHAPTER FIVE

Zack rubbed his hands together, eager to see Jada again. She fascinated him. Seeing her at her job the day before only made him want to get to know her that much more. He just hoped he didn't blow things with this first date. They had agreed to meet at Harvest Love, a nonprofit farm, one of the many charities he supported.

Thinking about his conversation with Donny, he had begun to have second thoughts about asking Jada out. Maybe Donny was right about her being high maintenance, and everything else Zack didn't want in his future wife. But he needed to find out for himself. The spark he felt between them told him that she was exactly what he wanted. She might have looked like she stepped off the cover of a fashion magazine at the reception, but in his gut he felt she was really down-to-earth. Besides, she had told him that she often did volunteer work. He couldn't think of a more worthy cause than helping to provide food to those who were down and out and needed a helping hand.

More and more volunteers were showing up, mostly women, but no Jada. Zack had called earlier, waking her up, and she assured him that she would be there.

Just then, he saw her pull into the parking lot and climb out of a champagne color Lexus with chrome rims and slightly tinted windows.

Even her car is sexy.

He watched as she put a few things into the trunk. His gaze immediately went to her *sweet ass*, admiring the way her tight designer jeans hugged her round butt. Although petite, Jada carried herself like a runway model.

Walking toward him, with each step she took, her long ponytail swung back and forth, making her look like a teenager, but Zack knew differently. The gentle sway of her curvaceous hips was as spellbinding as the first time he had seen her walk down the aisle at the wedding. The woman did wicked things to his body, and he had no doubt that they were a perfect match both mentally and physically.

He moved to meet her, and his gaze raked down her body analyzing the way she was dressed. Though she looked amazing in a fitted yellow T-shirt, tight dark jeans, and white tennis shoes, he was a little surprised that she didn't wear something a little less … nice.

He smiled when she removed her designer shades and squinted up at him.

"Hey beautiful," he said wrapping his arm around her back, kissing her on the cheek. The scent of her perfume, a combination of baby powder and flowers made him inhale deeply. Between her fragrance and the feel of her body against his, he didn't want to let her go. "I'm glad you could make it. Did you have any trouble finding the place?"

"A little. Once I exited the freeway, the stupid GPS had me going around in circles."

"That's why you should've let me pick you up. It wouldn't have been a problem."

"I appreciated the offer, but I didn't mind driving." She eased out of his grasp and glanced around. "This is not quite what I expected. This place is huge."

"Yeah, it is." He reached for her hand, glad that she

didn't pull away and led her to the main building. "It's over a hundred acres and as for produce, they grow everything from corn to strawberries. They also have horses back there," he pointed to a large red barn off in the distance, "and trails where people can go horseback riding or on hayrides."

"That's nice." She stumbled and gripped his hand tighter. Her focus now, mainly on each step as they walked across the uneven graveled lot. "I can't believe how hot it is already. It's barely seven in the morning."

"I'm surprised it's this warm in September. We usually get an earlier start in the summer to try and beat the heat."

"So you pack up produce for the farm often?"

"When my schedule allows." The only way he was able to be out there that early on a Saturday morning was because the team's weight-lifting practice had been pushed back to late afternoon. "This will probably be the last time I can get out here this year due to my football schedule. So I'm glad you were willing to join me." He opened the door to the building and followed her in. "I wasn't sure if you had eaten already, but they usually have breakfast for those interested."

"I'm not much of a breakfast person, but don't let me stop you."

They walked farther inside the warehouse-like building. Zack placed his hand at the small of her back and directed Jada to a set of long tables where people were still eating. Usually over fifty volunteers at any given time, many had already headed out to the gardens to get to work.

"Are you sure you don't want anything?" Zack pulled out a chair for her and held on to it until she was seated. "We'll be out in the field for a few hours. It'll probably take a lot out of you."

Jada stopped abruptly and narrowed her eyes at him. "Out in the field? As in picking vegetables in the dirt and mud?"

Zack grinned at the way her face twisted into a frown. "Uh, yeah. What did you expect?"

"You said that we would be boxing up fruits and veggies

for those less fortunate."

He nodded. "Yeah, that's part of it, but first we have to pick them."

***

"Oh, no, no, no, not me." Jada bolted from her seat making a mad dash toward the door. "I didn't sign up for all of this." Zack looped a long arm around her waist and halted her steps. He pulled her close, her backside rubbing against the front of his body.

"Don't tell me you're afraid of a little hard work." His warm breath caressed that spot behind her ear that always made her weak in the knees. Jada had no doubt that she would have puddled to the floor had he not been holding her up. "I promise you, it's not so bad." He turned her around to face him, and the tenderness of his smile lit up his face.

Ugh, those damn dimples.

What was he thinking? She didn't do dirt, and she hated sweating. Combine the two, and she certainly wasn't interested in digging in someone's garden. It was bad enough she had to do outdoor, physical labor for work.

Jada glanced at the passion pink color on her nails and shivered at the thought of ruining another manicure.

When Zack called to set up their date, she had expected an invite to a nice restaurant that Saturday night. Instead, he suggested a daytime date, volunteering for an organization she'd never heard of. She had her heart set on getting dressed up and going out on the town. But remembering their conversation on the dance floor a week earlier when she told him she often did volunteer work, she could see why he'd come up with the idea.

"Say that you'll stay." His arm rested around her shoulders as he led her back to the table and onto her chair. "Besides, spending this time together will give us a chance to get to know each other better."

They could have gotten to know each other over dinner at Nicola's, one of her favorite restaurants she wanted to say.

Yet, when he placed his hand on her back, her thoughts jumbled inside her head. How could a simple touch from him send her senses into overdrive?

"So if I leave you here alone, will you promise not to try and escape?"

She didn't bother to glance up at him, knowing that she'd be defenseless against his eyes and his smile. "Yeah, yeah, I promise."

He chuckled and squeezed her shoulder. "Okay, then I'll be back in a second. I'm going to grab some breakfast." She watched him stroll away, his gait easy like that of a self-confident man, comfortable in his skin.

Jada glanced around, her gaze immediately traveling to the ceiling. The first thing she noticed when stepping into any room, since becoming a sheet metal worker, was the ductwork and the heating and air conditioning vents. She hated filthy vents. Not only did they look bad, dirt build up on them meant filters weren't being changed often enough, resulting in poor air quality. In a huge space like this, it was hard to see the condition of the vents, which were at least twenty feet from the floor. But she loved that the owners kept the metal ductwork exposed, where many chose to paint theirs or add a drop ceiling.

Zack returned moments later, and his plates were loaded with food. The tantalizing scent of bacon, eggs, and toast tickled her nose. She wasn't hungry, but the aroma and how good everything looked, had her wanting to grab his fork and dig into his food.

"Are you really going to eat all of that?"

"Yep, unless you want some of it."

Jada shook her head. "Nah, I'm good. Thanks."

Zack left and came back with coffee for her and juice for himself. They talked and laughed like old friends. Most Saturdays, Jada spent shopping or hanging out with her family. Spending time with Zack was proving to be a nice change.

Fifteen minutes later, he was finished eating. "Ready to get started?" he asked.

"I'm about as ready as I'll ever be."

Jada couldn't believe he had eaten everything on his plates. Dancing with him weeks ago, she could tell he was in excellent shape. If he ate like that all the time, she couldn't imagine what type of strenuous workout routine he had. She immediately envisioned him shirtless with toned muscles covered in perspiration gliding down his broad chest. His muscles rippling against her hand as she ran her fingers across his six-pack and down his…

Whoa! Jada blew out a breath to slow the rapid beat of her heart. *Don't even go there.* Those types of lustful thoughts could easily get her into trouble. She was looking for marriage, not love. She had been down that road before and vowed, never again. Never would she open herself up to a man only to have him step on her feelings and treat her like she was nothing. Never would she think a few nice gifts equaled love, and never would she allow a man anywhere near her heart again.

Zack stood, gathered his plates, and tossed them in a nearby trashcan. "Are you sure that cup of coffee is going to be enough for you?" he asked, offering Jada a hand to help her to her feet.

"Yep, I'm still not hungry. I'll get something when we finish here."

His eyebrows scrunched together. Concern showed in his crystal blue eyes. She could easily get lost in those eyes and could barely draw her gaze from his whenever he looked at her.

"It's going to get very hot out in the field."

Heck, it's already hot just standing next to you, she thought.

"I just don't want to take a chance on you getting too hungry or dehydrated out there. Besides that, do you have a hat?"

She almost laughed. She rarely wore hats, especially in the summer. The last thing she wanted to do was sweat out her relaxer. Besides, unlike him, the dark pigment of her skin provided her a little more protection from the sun. Instead of telling Zack that or why she didn't wear hats, Jada grabbed her empty coffee cup and tossed it in the trash as they headed to the door.

"Don't worry. I'll be fine." She slipped on her Dolce and Gabbana sunglasses, shielding her eyes from the bright sun when they stepped outside.

As Zack grabbed a few oversized baskets from a large bin, he explained that they would need them for carrying the vegetables.

"How did you get involved with Harvest Love?"

"Come this way." Zack held her hand and led the way to the back of the building. "Being raised by a single parent, money was tight. My mom did the best she could and for the most part, I had a decent childhood," he shrugged, "but there were times when she found herself in between jobs and had to seek out food banks. Harvest Love was one of them. And like many kids who grew up poor, I vowed that when I made a little money, I would give back."

Listening to Zack talk about his childhood and his mother's financial troubles during that time made Jada appreciate her grandfather that much more. Thanks to his fortitude and entrepreneurial spirit, Jenkins & Sons Construction provided work for anyone in the family who wanted a job. Though she didn't plan on working in construction for the rest of her life, she knew most of her cousins loved their jobs.

"Have you ever picked cucumbers?" Zack's question invaded her thoughts. They neared a field with rows and rows of plants. Had he not said anything, she wouldn't know a cucumber plant from a tomato plant.

"No, I can honestly say this is a first for me." Even with both her mother and grandmother having gardens, Jada never had an interest.

Zack squeezed her hand. "Well, hopefully this will be the first of many for us."

Hell, if this is what he thought of as a fun date, there wouldn't be anymore anything for them because this would be the last time she'd go out with him.

They stopped at the edge of the field. Scratching her arm and then her leg, Jada wasn't sure if she were allergic to something out there, or if the itching was all in her head. The thought of digging around in the dirt was making her break out in hives.

I so don't want to do this. She enjoyed eating, but never thought about the work involved in getting the food from the farm to the dinner table.

She followed Zack, tiptoeing to keep her white tennis shoes from getting too dirty. A sick feeling rolled around in her stomach. She'd paid a small fortune for the white leather Gucci shoes just last week. This was her first time wearing them and by the looks of the ground, she was pretty sure she wouldn't be able to wear them again.

It's not always about you, Jada.

Her grandfather's words popped into her mind. Maybe if she just focused on the reason she was out there, to help feed the needy, she could take her mind off the tennis shoes. Just then, her foot sunk down into the mud and a small scream caught in her throat.

Oh, damn, damn, damn!

Some of the growl rolling around in her throat must have slipped through because Zack stopped and turned back to her.

"You okay?" He extended his hand to help her walk, but she ignored the gesture. If she grabbed hold of his hand, she might try to break his bones with the anger bubbling inside of her.

Who takes a person on a first date to a stupid farm? She didn't get a chance to ask. The words died in her throat when

Zack lowered his hand and snaked his arm around her waist. The heat from his touch skirted through her body, short-circuiting all thoughts, which only made her more frustrated. One minute she wanted to give him a piece of her mind, and then the next she wanted to be hugged up against him.

"Be careful." He guided her around a couple of puddles. "We'll start over there since it's not as muddy."

Why'd he have to be so darn nice? If he were a jerk, it would be real easy to leave him, his baskets and cucumbers out there in the hot sun. Instead, his kindness weakened her resolve and made her want to help.

Zack released her and set down the bushel baskets. He pulled two pair of gloves from his back pocket and handed a set to her and then he slipped on the others. Squatting in front of a bush, he glanced back at her.

"Here, come a little closer." He moved over some when she stood next to him. "To pick the cucumbers, hold the stem with one hand like this." He demonstrated. "Then pull the vegetable with the other." He picked a few and then placed them in one of the baskets. "They mature pretty fast. So someone is usually picking them every other day. With that said though, if they are at least this size," he held up one that was about six or seven inches long, "make sure you don't pass by it. Otherwise, if they get too big, the plants will stop producing."

Zack schooled Jada on the do's and don'ts of picking vegetables, impressing her with his knowledge of gardening. He shared more than she cared to know, but she had to admit the information was a little interesting. Thirty minutes into their task, Zack insisted she stand upright, claiming that picking cucumbers were murder on the back.

"Every few minutes take a couple of seconds to stretch. Otherwise, you'll regret you didn't later."

They worked and talked. Before long Jada realized the experience wasn't as bad as she first thought it would be. No, she would never be able to wear her new tennis shoes again, and no she couldn't see herself digging in dirt ever again, but she was enjoying her time with Zack. A perfect gentleman, he helped her whenever needed, keeping her entertained, and she found their conversation engaging.

"Ahhh!" Jada screamed and fell back on her butt, throwing down the cucumbers. She leaped up and shook her hands frantically, sending the gloves flying off into the plants. "Ugh! Oh my God!"

"What?" Zack jumped up and grabbed her arm. "What is it?"

Jada's eyes flickered over her body, holding a hand against her chest, she tried to slow her racing heart. Nerves on edge, she took a few deep breaths. She wasn't afraid of worms or bugs, but she hated them.

"Jada?"

Looking up she met Zack's worried gaze, his hand still on her arm. Blowing out a loud breath, all she could do was shake her head. *He must think I'm a total goof.*

"A worm fell onto my glove."

Zack looked at her as if she had lost her mind. He dropped his hand from her arm. Removing his glove, he ran his fingers through his dark, spiked hair. "Why didn't you tell me you were afraid of worms?"

"I'm not," she said defensively.

"Then what was the screaming about? What else are you afraid of?"

"Nothing! The worm just caught me off guard, and I freaked. Forgive me. It's been awhile since I've dug around in dirt!" She knew she sounded like a crazy person, but at the moment, she didn't care. He was the idiot who had talked her into hanging out at the farm.

She dropped down on her knees, slipped her gloves on, and went back to work, ignoring him. *This is what I get for pretending to be a person who loves the outdoors and who enjoys gardening.*

Stupid, stupid, stupid.

They worked in silence for a while until Zack spoke up. "Listen, I'm sorry if I seemed insensitive a few minutes ago." He yanked on one of the vines and pulled a cucumber off. "*You* caught me off guard and *I* freaked. So I can see how a worm could do the same to you."

Jada tossed a couple of cucumbers in the basket closest to her and sat back on her haunches. She swiped the back of her gloved hand across her forehead and smiled at him.

"I'm sorry I overreacted." She laughed and shook her head. "I'm sure I looked pretty crazy tripping out over a worm. It just came out of nowhere."

"Don't apologize. It could've happened to anyone. I'm just glad you're not afraid of them or bugs. Otherwise, this bright idea of mine to have our first date here, wouldn't have been a good idea." He picked up her empty bottle of water. "Want some more?"

"Nah, I'm good."

Feeling beads of sweat roll down her back, she couldn't wait to jump in the shower. Maybe she should have taken Zack up on his offer to wear one of his hats. At least then it wouldn't feel as if her head was on fire. The sun shone brightly, and the temperature was steadily rising.

"Are you doing all right?" He stood and studied her. "Do you need a break? That one bottle of water is not enough for handling this heat out here."

"I'm okay." She was a little thirsty, and she could eat, but she didn't want to stop. She had already had coffee that morning, and had knocked out that bottle of water a few minutes ago. Anything else to drink and she would be running to the bathroom. They were on a roll, and she knew if she stopped, that would probably be the end for her.

"Well, just let me know when you need to stop."

They went back to work, their conversation flowing easily.

"You mentioned that your brothers used to hunt and fish with your grandfather when they were younger. What about you? Did you go fishing with them?"

Jada cringed at the thought. There was no way they would have gotten her out there to hang around waiting for fish to bite. Besides, the way her brothers smelled by the time they walked through the door was enough to turn her off from the idea.

Instead of giving Zack her honest opinion, she said, "No, that was their way of doing guy things together. No women allowed." She tossed a couple of cucumbers in the basket and stood. She had filled four baskets so far and was hoping to do at least ten before calling it a day. "I take it you do the whole fishing, hunting, hiking thing."

"Yep." Zack stood and removed his baseball cap, and his dark hair was plastered to his head. He swiped his forearm across his forehead and replaced the cap. "Sunshine, rain, snow, or sleet, it doesn't matter. I like being out in the fresh air."

"So what else do you enjoy doing?" Jada asked.

"Ah, let's see. I like sleeping in on Sunday mornings and reading the newspaper when I don't have a game. I would travel more if I had time, and I also enjoy shopping."

"Get out of here." Jada leaned back, checking him out to see if he was serious. "You're telling me, you, a man, enjoy shopping? I can't believe it."

"Believe it, but don't get me wrong. I hate malls. I usually do my shopping either through a personal shopper or online. I have a weakness for rugged boots and tennis shoes."

I think I'm in love. A man who loves to shop. That explains his hiking boots being a perfect match to his dark mustard colored T-shirt.

"And like you," Zack continued, "I love playing video games. Although unlike you, I prefer the ones where I get to blow up things."

Jada laughed. "Figures. My male cousins insist that a video game isn't a game if you can't blow up something. I still say the racing games are the best."

As they moved down the cucumber rows, she realized they had more in common than she originally thought. It wasn't until he started talking about fishing and some of his favorite hiking trails that their differences became apparent.

Jada couldn't remember the last time she laughed and held a regular conversation with a guy. Such a simple thing was standing out to her as something that should have been the norm. Most of the men she dated talked about their work, or the latest deal they had closed. But Zack was different. So far, they had talked about everything from family to favorite vacation spots.

Jada opened her mouth to complain about the sun beating down on her neck, but she kept her mouth closed. It was okay to complain around her family, they knew her, but she didn't want to come across as a complainer to Zack. She wasn't sure why his opinion of her mattered, especially since she had no intention of going out with him again, but it did.

There were only a few people working in their row, but she did notice a man in the next aisle who kept staring at them.

"Do you know that guy over there?" Jada asked nodding toward the man in the tan Indiana Jones hat. "He looks as if he's trying to get your attention."

Zack sighed. "I'm trying to ignore him," he said without looking over to see who she was referring to. "I agreed to autograph his football before I leave today. He's probably making sure I don't duck out without following through."

"Wow, you can't even hide out in a vegetable field without your fans finding you, huh?"

He turned to look at her, his eyes shielded by slick aviator sunglasses. The corner of his lip tilted up in a grin. "Yeah, no matter where I go they seem to find me. But this is the first time in a long time that a fan has spotted me out here. I guess not too many of them volunteer on farms." Jada didn't miss the sarcasm dripping from each word and assumed he didn't like the attention.

"I take it this guy is not a regular volunteer." She tossed a couple of cucumbers into the basket and slipped off her gloves and then her sunglasses. She dabbed at the sweat on her nose and under her eyes with the back of her wrist. Normally she didn't walk out of the house without her makeup being applied perfectly, but she was pretty sure her efforts had been in vain considering how much she'd been wiping her face.

"His wife is a regular. I guess she told him that I volunteered here sometime."

"So have you ever refused a person an autograph?"

"A couple of times." He added a few cucumbers to one basket that was overflowing, and dropped the rest into hers. "I think there are appropriate times and places for autographs. I don't like it when someone interrupts me while I'm on a date or eating, to ask for an autograph. If I'm just hanging out with the guys at a bar or something like that, then it's not as big of a deal."

Personally, Jada enjoyed attention but had a feeling the type of attention he drew would get old real quick.

"Here, let me swap out your full basket for this empty one. I'm going to start taking these containers to the drop off spot. I'll be right back." He removed his sunglasses and let them hang from his neck.

"Okay." Jada stood but before she could say anything else, she staggered to the side, her head feeling a little loopy.

"Whoa." Zack dropped the basket and caught her by the arm before she toppled over. "You okay?"

Blinking rapidly, Jada shook her head hoping to clear up the blurriness. She leaned into Zack.

"What's wrong?" He lifted her chin with his finger, forcing her to look at him. The concern she saw in those big baby-blues made her heart flip. She didn't know what was more attractive, his gorgeous eyes or those dimples he flashed every so often, making her knees weak. But right now he wasn't smiling.

Jada inhaled and then slowly released the breath. "That was weird, but I'm fine. I think I just stood up too fast."

"Nah, I think it's more than that." Zack wrapped his arm around her waist. "We've been at this a few hours. I think we should take a break so you can get something to drink *and* something to eat. The little water you had almost an hour ago isn't enough to keep you hydrated out here."

"Zack, I told you, I'm fine." She pulled away, still feeling a little light-headed, but sure, she could stand on her own. "I want to fill up a few more baskets before I stop. You said your goal was to fill at least ten of them before lunch, and I plan to do the same."

"No. We're stopping now." He placed his hand on her elbow prepared to guide her out of the field, but she yanked her arm from his grasp.

Jada had to keep herself from giving him one of her signature neck rolls. Instead, she put her hands on her hips and looked at him pointedly. She wasn't used to anyone saying no to her and she sure as hell didn't like anyone telling her what to do.

"I'm a grown woman. I'll let you know when I need a break."

"Jada." He sighed in exasperation. He removed his cap and swiped at the perspiration on his forehead. "I'm not trying to boss you around. It's hot out here, and I'm just looking out for you, especially since you haven't eaten anything."

"Would you just go? The sooner you take those baskets and come back with empty ones, the sooner we can get done."

He still didn't seem convinced, but Jada ignored him. It wasn't until she heard him leave did she look up. Despite still feeling a little lightheaded, she couldn't help but admire his nice butt.

Whew, that is one fine man.

She smiled and shook her head, immediately regretting the sudden move when she felt her body waver again.

"Okay Jada, get it together."

She lowered herself and knelt on her hands and knees. Closing her eyes, she breathed in slowly, then exhaled. There had been plenty of times she had gone longer than a few hours without food and water, never having a problem. The only difference she could think of is that she was outside in the hot sun, but still…

Maybe Zack's right. Maybe it is time to take a break.

She'd take a couple of minutes to get herself together before heading to the main building for some water. She just hoped Zack wasn't one of those guys who said, "I told you so." Normally she knew her body, but of course, it would betray her now that she was out with a hot guy.

A few minutes passed and she felt a little steadier. She sat back and removed her gloves, then her sunglasses. The only time she hung outside when it was that hot was if she were working. Yet she'd not only let the blue-eyed hottie talk her into working outdoors, but she'd also allowed him to convince her to pick vegetables. She smiled to herself. Her cousins were never going to believe she'd done some gardening.

Feeling a little better, she stood slowly, but a bout of dizziness gripped her. *Oh God.* She staggered. Panic lodged in her throat as her heart rate spiked. Blinking her eyes several times, she couldn't fight the blurriness. Her body teetered left, then right. There was nothing to grab. Everything around her spun in circles.

"Zack." The whisper slipped through her lips before everything went black.

CHAPTER SIX

Zack carried the baskets full of cucumbers into the main building and handed them off, still berating himself about not taking more breaks. Used to working in the field alone, he went hours before stopping. With this being Jada's first time out there, and she hadn't eaten, he should've known better. She might think she's fine, but she didn't look fine.

I should've insisted on her eating something before we went out there.

He stuffed two bottles of water into his back pockets and headed back outside to grab a couple of empty baskets. He had to admit he was enjoying Jada's company. She was down to earth with a witty sense of humor. He also liked the way she went with the flow. Thinking about a couple of the women he had dated over the years, there was no way any of them would be caught dead in a field working.

I knew she was different.

Zack neared the edge of the field when he saw a few people hurrying to the row where he had left Jada. What he didn't see was Jada. It wasn't until the guy who had asked for his autograph started waving his arms frantically did a sinking feeling settle in his gut.

Oh damn.

Zack dropped the baskets and took off in a sprint, his heart pounding wildly in his chest. He didn't know what was going on, but he knew something was wrong.

"Move, move!" He pushed his way through the small crowd. "Jada?" She was laying on the ground, a towel under her head. Zack knelt down next to her. "What the hell happened?"

The guy who wanted the autograph spoke up. "When I was over there," he pointed to the next row, "I noticed she looked a little disoriented, but before I could ask if she was alright, she collapsed."

"Jada? Sweetheart?" Zack touched her clammy cheek and noticed a small bruise near her hairline. He hadn't noticed it before and assumed she'd gotten it when she passed out. She moaned, and her eyes fluttered, but she didn't open them.

"I need to get her out of this sun," he mumbled more to himself than anyone else. He lifted her into his arms and held her close. "Mrs. Conner, would you find Doc and ask him to meet me in Grady's office?" She agreed, and Zack rushed toward the main building.

"I'll grab her things for you," the autograph guy said of Jada's sunglasses and gloves.

Zack didn't give a damn about that stuff. All he wanted was to get Jada inside the air-conditioned building and get some liquids into her. He was pretty sure she was dehydrated but he needed the doctor to confirm his suspicions.

Kicking open the door to the main building, Zack hurried to the back hallway that led to Mr. Grady, the farm owner's, office. He flew past the kitchen, bathrooms, and a supply closet. "Grady!" he called out when he got closer. "Grady!"

"I can walk," Jada mumbled. "I don't need some big, sexy guy…" Her words trailed off, and Zack got more concerned. He felt better hearing her talk, at least then he knew she was okay.

The door at the end of the hall swung open, and Grady

stood in the doorway. He snatched off his reading glasses. "What's going on?" He rushed forward when he saw Zack carrying Jada. "What happened?"

"She fainted. I need to lay her down." Zack moved around Grady, not waiting for permission to enter the office and went straight to a leather sofa at the back of the small room. He laid her down, placing a pillow under her head. He removed her muddy shoes and shoved a pillow under her feet. "I asked Mrs. Conner to find Doc, can you—"

Jada groaned, and her eyes eased open.

"Jada?" Zack sat on the side of the sofa, his hand cupping her cheek. "Sweetheart, can you hear me?" She swallowed and then tried to sit up. He placed his hand on her shoulder to keep her down. "No, you need to just lay here for a few minutes."

Staring into each other's eyes, Zack brushed her hair away from her face, the back of his fingers lingering against her soft cheek. *There is something about this woman*. Each time his gaze met hers, his heart turned over in response.

A noise behind him snapped him out of his trance.

"She needs some water." He reached for the bottles of water in his back pockets, but they must have fallen out at some point. Before he could turn to Grady, a bottle was in his hands. "Jada, you need to drink something." Zack snatched the top off, letting it fall to the floor and lifted her head.

"Mmm, no. I'm tired," she mumbled, her eyes closed. She pulled away from him, swatting at the hand that held the bottle.

"I know, sweetheart, but I need you to drink this." Zack moved his hand to the back of her head to hold her still and practically poured water into her mouth. She coughed a little, and the moment she stopped, he poured more water into her mouth until she drunk on her own.

"Hey Grady, what happened?" Doc asked when he stepped into the doorway. His long, salt and pepper hair pulled back and bound at the back of his neck was covered with a wide straw hat, which he removed and laid on the table.

"Over here," Zack said. "She passed out. I think she's dehydrated, but I want to make sure nothing else is going on."

"Here, let me take a look." Doc dropped his gloves on the table near his hat and quickly washed his hands at the small wet bar in the corner of the room. He moved back to where Jada laid, dragged a chair over to the sofa, and asked a series of questions.

Jada mumbled that she didn't need a doctor. As far as Zack was concerned, the fact that she wasn't trying to get up spoke volumes.

The doctor checked her vitals, a bruise at the hairline close to her ear, and another on the back of her head.

"Besides the two bruises, there doesn't seem to be any other injuries," Doc said to Jada. "You have a slight temperature, but I think it's from being in the hot sun. You're definitely dehydrated so try to drink plenty of liquids over the next hour, and you should be fine, maybe a little tired, but fine nonetheless."

Glad that she was going to be okay, Zack's heart rate had finally gone back to normal. Finding her lying on the ground scared him to death, and he knew he never wanted to experience anything like that again.

When Doc and Grady left, Zack held Jada's hand and sighed. *This was one heck of a first date.* Now he just hoped he could talk her into a second one.

"Is she okay?"

Zack jerked his head toward the doorway where the autograph guy was standing.

"She will be. She just got a little dehydrated." Zack turned back to Jada, who had her eyes closed, and he gently touched her cheek.

"So what about my football, can you still sign it?"

"Not right now," Zack muttered. Just that fast he'd forgotten that the guy was standing there.

"But you said—"

"Are you fucking kidding me, man?" Zack bolted from his seat and got into the guy's face. His anger went from zero to sixty in seconds. He couldn't believe some people. "My girl is sick and you're asking me about a damn football."

"Hey, you're the one who said that you'd give me your autographed. When I saw you leave the field, I figured you were getting ready to leave."

"Zack." Jada's soft voice floated through the air. He left the man standing at the door not giving a damn about an autograph or anything else for that matter, except for Jada.

"Hey." Zack dropped down next to her. "Want something else to drink?" He grabbed the second bottle of Gatorade that he had received from Grady earlier. Opening the bottle, he helped her sit up and then handed it to Jada.

She shook her head. "I don't—"

"Nah, you need to drink some more. You're still a little dehydrated, and this is going to help replenish some of the salt your body lost."

"Zack…" She started to lay back down, but Zack stopped her.

"I need you to drink some of this so you'll feel better. Then I'll take you home."

The guy at the door cleared his throat. Zack shot daggers at him with his eyes. "I'm not doing that right now. You can either come back some other time or leave the football with Grady, and I'll sign it when I can." Zack returned his attention to Jada but heard the man spout out a few curse words before he moved away from the door.

Jada slumped against Zack. "I'm so tired." He wrapped his arms around her and placed a kiss against her temple. It wasn't until she winced did he remember her bruise.

"Oh, shoot, sorry about that. You must have hit the side

of your head when you passed out. Does your head hurt?"

"A little, but I've been told – on more than one occasion – I have a hard head."

Though she said it with a straight face, Zack chuckled, glad to see her sense of humor was still intact.

"You almost gave me a heart attack out there." He thought about her mumbling when he carried her into the office. "So did you mean it when you said that I was sexy?"

She stared at him and lifted her small hand to his face, her thumb rubbing over his stubble. "Um, I don't remember," she said unconvincingly and glanced away. He placed his hand on top of hers, bringing her attention back to him. "Thanks for taking care of me." Her words spoken so quietly he barely heard her, but he didn't miss the desire gleaming in her pretty brown eyes.

All it would take is for both of them to move their heads forward a few inches, and their lips would connect. Zack ached to kiss her but debated with himself, not wanting to move too fast and scare her away.

To hell with it.

He eased forward and lowered his head. When her breathing hitched, he froze and met her gaze. Not until she gave a small smile did he go in for what he wanted. He cupped the back of her neck and brushed his lips against hers. All day he'd wanted to taste those sweet lips, and it had definitely been worth the wait. His heart stuttered when her lips parted and he took the small gesture as an invitation, slipping his tongue into her mouth. She clung to his upper arms. Their tongues tangled and it was at that moment Zack knew that this would not be their last date.

Zack could have kissed her for the rest of the day, but when her hands framed his face, she slowly ended their kiss. He wasn't ready to let her go and rested his forehead against hers.

"I guess by now you're probably hungry."

"Yes, I am."

Placing a chaste kiss against her cheek, he said, "All right then. Let's get out of here. We'll stop and get you something to eat before I take you home."

Zack helped her stand. When she didn't seem too steady on her feet, he wrapped his arm around her waist.

"Wait. I can't leave my car here," Jada said when they stepped outside.

"I'll take care of it. But right now I'm more concerned about taking care of you."

***

As Zack drove, Jada thought about the sweet kiss they had shared. His tenderness was enough to melt her heart and make her yearn for more. But it was good they'd stopped. A little bit more and that kiss would have spun out of control and possibly led to something else.

Now, almost home, she kept thinking about her car being left at the farm. She was too tired to argue about leaving it and too tired to drive. She still couldn't believe she had fainted, but was glad that Zack hadn't said, "I told you so."

"Why aren't you eating? Do you want something from someplace else?" Zack asked. Even though she had snacked on Trail Mix, he had stopped by Dewey's, one of her favorite pizza joints, and ordered her a cheese and sausage pizza to go. The enticing aroma coming from the pizza box in the back seat was making her hungrier.

"I figured I'd wait until I got home, less messy." Jada fiddled with her purse strap. "I'm sorry about all of this and cutting your time short at the farm. I should have listened when you suggested we take a break, but I thought the light-headiness would pass."

Zack grabbed hold of her hand and squeezed. "Don't even worry about it. I'm just glad you're feeling better. I'm sure after you eat something and get some rest, you'll be back to normal."

She hoped so. Later that night she had a date with Marcus, the CEO of a bank, who she had met a few months earlier. He had canceled the last two dates because of work, and she was looking forward to getting dressed up and going out.

A short while later, Zack pulled up to Christina's house. Shutting off the engine, he turned to face her.

"Are you sure you're okay? You don't need to go to the hospital?"

Jada shook her head, still feeling a slight ache on the side of her forehead. "I'll be fine."

"Thanks for being such a trooper today. I know you were concerned about us not reaching the goal I had set, but we got a lot done. Typically, for every full basket of fruits and vegetables collected, three families will receive enough fresh produce to last a couple of weeks. You did great. There were a lot of volunteers out there today so I have no doubt that many families will receive some assistance."

Despite having ruined a brand new pair of tennis shoes, broken a nail, and then passing out from heat exhaustion, Jada felt good in knowing that she helped someone in need. She could see why people did volunteer work. Even without knowing who would receive the boxes of food, she knew a family wouldn't go hungry because of the work she did that day.

"Thanks for inviting me. It's been awhile since I've done any volunteer work, and I'm glad you suggested we help out today. It wasn't so bad." She smiled when his eyebrows shot upward as if he didn't believe her. "Seriously, it wasn't. If ever I do something like that again, I'll make sure I drink plenty of water and eat breakfast."

"Good. I'm glad to know that I didn't scare you away." Jada didn't have the heart to tell him she had no intention of digging in anyone's garden no time soon.

He climbed out of the truck and walked around to the passenger side. Grabbing the pizza from the back seat, he opened her door and helped her out.

"If you give me your car keys," he said walking her to the

door, "I'll have your car delivered as well as another little surprise to you within the hour."

Her heart sang with delight. She loved surprises and thought it sweet of him to take care of her car. She could have easily gotten one of her cousins to go back out to the farm with her later that day. Yet, she was glad she didn't have to. As for the surprise he had for her, she just hoped it wasn't more purple tools.

After seeing Zack off, Jada walked into the house and closed the door. Placing her handbag on the table in the entryway, she kicked off her muddy tennis shoes. Relief flowed through her as she walked farther into the house with the pizza box, happy to be home.

Jada stopped short. "What?" Christina stood frozen in the middle of the hallway, staring at her.

"What happened to you?"

"What do you mean?" She glanced down at herself, knowing that her clothes were a little dirty, but the way Christina was looking at her one would think Jada had two heads.

Christina continued staring at her before she burst out laughing. "Are you serious? You come in here with a streak of dirt across your face, hair standing on top of your head, and filthy clothes and think nothing of it? What's wrong with you and what have you done with my superficial, vain cousin?"

Anyone else would have taken offense to the insult, but not Jada. She was more concerned about what Christina saw when she looked at her.

Jada narrowed her eyes at her cousin and shoved the pizza box into her hands. She hurried into the half bath on the first floor, turned on the light and stood before the full-length mirror.

"Oh my God!" she screamed, her hands flying to her hair and then her face. "I look a hot mess!" Most of her hair had come out of her ponytail holder and looked as if birds had made a nest on top of her head. And the dirt that CJ had referred to was mud that had dried on her face. Not only had she ruined her tennis shoes, but the expensive yellow T-shirt might never come clean.

She stormed out of the bathroom and ran up the stairs, ignoring her hunger pains and CJ's laughter that followed behind her. If Jada ever saw Zack again, she was going to ring his neck. How could he let her walk around looking like a crack head?

She hurried out of her clothes, leaving them by the door of the attached bathroom and stepped into the shower.

"Who takes a first date to a stupid farm?" Jada said as she lathered with her favorite lavender body wash. Even after a full day of hanging ductwork, she didn't get this dirty.

She had a few hours to recharge and get ready for a real date with Marcus. At least with him she could dress up in her new dress and stilettos. And she was guaranteed a meal at a five-star restaurant.

Her thoughts went back to Zack, and a warm glow flew through her. She hated picking vegetables, but had to admit. If she were going to do something like gardening again with anyone, she would want it to be with him. In his element out there, he conquered weeds and protected her from worms and spiders. She didn't miss how everyone gravitated to him, not because of him being a professional football player, but because he was a genuinely nice guy.

Five hours later, Jada felt like a new woman. If she thought Zack was a nice guy earlier, she now thought he was a real sweetheart. True to his word, her car had arrived within an hour, and the surprise showed up. Best gift ever – a masseuse to work out the kinks in her tired muscles. Jada pampered herself regularly but never had a massage left her so rejuvenated like the one that afternoon. The woman worked her magical fingers on Jada's sore muscles, leaving her feeling refreshed and ready for anything.

Now she had a few minutes to finish getting ready for her

date with Marcus. She strode into her walk-in closet and slipped into the purple matching bra and pantie set that she had purchased from La Perla. The items might have cost her a day's wage, but would go perfect with her dress. From the moment she had hit puberty, she insisted that her underwear match whatever outfit she wore, driving her mother crazy.

She glanced at the clock. *Fifteen minutes left.* Always prompt, Marcus would be ringing the doorbell at any minute. Hurrying, she stepped into the purple one-shoulder Ralph Lauren dress and smoothed her hands down the side of her body, loving the way the silky material hugged her figure. The color looked amazing against her brown skin and enhanced the sparkle of her dangling diamond earrings with the matching necklace.

The doorbell rang.

"Right on time." She slipped into her matching four-inch pumps to complete the outfit.

Jada took one last look in the mirror and grabbed her purse. Seconds later, she stood at the top of the stairs, waiting for Christina to call her down. Jada always liked to make an entrance for her dates, and since CJ didn't seem to mind getting the door, Jada took advantage of the opportunity. Before she took a step, her cell phone chimed signaling a text message.

I HAD A GREAT TIME TODAY. I LOOK FORWARD TO THE NEXT TIME I SEE YOU. ZACK.

She hadn't agreed to go out with him again, and if she did, the date would have to involve something less dirty. Yet, she had to admit that the gift of a massage would go down as one of the sweetest gifts ever. Now she understood how professional football players were able to recover so quickly after playing a hard game. She felt as if she could party all night.

Jada glided down the stairs slowly, to ensure that Marcus got a good look. Her gaze connected with Christina's, who stood at the bottom of the stairs, prepared to holler her name again. Her cousin grinned and shook her head. She thought that Jada spent way too much money on clothes and shoes. Her cousin didn't understand, that in order for Jada to attract the type of man she was looking to marry, she had to invest in clothes, shoes and handbags.

"Oh, here she is," Christina said to Marcus and disappeared into the living room.

Marcus reached for her hand to help her down the last three steps. "I don't know how it's possible, but I think you get more beautiful every time I see you."

Jada beamed. "You're so sweet. Thank you." She did a quick glance at his dark blue tailored suit with the small gray pinstripes, his gray shirt, and the designer tie. He looked every bit the banker. "You look pretty amazing yourself. Did you have to work today?"

"I did, but you know, I work pretty much every day."

She remembered. The number of work hours he put in was probably the one thing she didn't like about him. Cancelling a couple of dates with her because of work obligations didn't go over well. She was all for a man making money, but she didn't appreciate coming second to someone's job.

"Shall we go?"

"I'm ready." She slipped her arm through his bent arm, and he guided her to the door. "CJ, I'm gone. Don't wait up." She didn't wait for a response, and they stepped out into the warm, fall night.

Two hours later, Jada sat across from Marcus sipping a glass of white wine, slouching in her seat. If he talked any more about bank stuff or how great he was on the golf course the day before she was going to throw a plate at him.

"Can I get the two of you anything else? Maybe dessert?" the server asked as she cleared away their dinner dishes.

"No, thanks. My dessert for the evening is sitting across from me," Marcus said, flashing his beautiful smile. Too bad Jada wasn't feeling him or his pretty white teeth. She couldn't understand how a perfectly packaged man could be such a bore.

"Nothing for me, thank you," Jada said sweetly.

Marcus caressed her hand, his touch more irritating than sensual. "Why don't we go back to my penthouse for a nightcap … and dessert?"

She squeezed his hand before slipping hers from his grasp. Sitting back in her seat, she debated on how to play the next few minutes. She'd had dinner at his place a couple of times and loved being surrounded by such luxury. Before tonight, she thought Marcus was potential marriage material despite the twenty year age difference, but now, all she wanted to do was get away from him.

"You know what? Why don't we call it a night? I've had a super long day and volunteering at the farm has worn me out." Tonight she didn't have to feign exhaustion. It had been a long day.

"Since when did you start volunteering anywhere, especially on a farm?" Marcus lifted the glass of Cognac to his lips and sipped. "Isn't that a little beneath you? Especially since I remember you saying something about having an adverse reaction to dirt."

Jada ignored the funky attitude behind his words. "Doing something to help those less fortunate is not beneath me. Granted I don't like getting dirty, but I have to admit, it felt good to do something for someone else." She thought about Zack and his reasons for volunteering on the farm. She wondered if she sounded as snobbish as Marcus did when she all but turned her nose up at the idea originally.

They left the restaurant and the more she talked about her time with Zack, the more she realized she actually had a good time.

"So what prompted you to volunteer?" Marcus merged onto I-275, which had more traffic than usual for that time of night. "I just can't see you doing it willingly. With the wealth your family has, I'd think you'd just write a check."

Did he really think that little of her? And her grandparents were wealthy. Heck, she barely had enough in her checking account to buy a sandwich. The conversation with Marcus tonight made her recognize just how little they knew about each other, but she could see how her usual attitude would warrant his questions.

"A friend of mine does a lot of volunteering and asked if I'd be interested in tagging along."

He chuckled. "*You* have friends who do volunteer work? The way you talk, all you guys usually do is shop."

Jada turned slightly in her seat. "If you think so little of me, why ask me out and send me gifts?"

Marcus shrugged. "Honestly?" He glanced at her and returned his attention back to the road. "You're a beautiful woman. With the type of people I associate with, and the connections I'm trying to make, I need a woman who looks good on my arm. Besides, we've been having a good time or at least I have. I even figured after tonight that we'd take our relationship to the next level."

"And what exactly is the next level?"

"Well, my plan was for us to have a nice dinner, and then hang out at my place. We'd listen to a little jazz, have a nightcap, and maybe see where the evening goes from there." He smiled, and the twinkle in his eyes making it clear what else he had in mind.

The more time Jada spent with him, the more disinterested she became. They'd gone out maybe six or seven times and as far as she was concerned, she hadn't thought too much about going to the next level. Yes, he was handsome, wealthy, and had amazing taste in jewelry, but outside of that – nothing. She felt absolutely nothing. There were no unique outings, no entertaining conversations, and no lustful thoughts, stirring in her gut.

Not like with Zack.

Before today, that might've been okay, but spending only a few hours with Zack made her see how much she enjoyed good conversation with a man.

They pulled up to Jada's place, and she couldn't get away from Marcus fast enough. She just hated she had wasted so much time with him.

Marcus parked, and Jada stopped him before he opened his door.

"You know what? Why don't we say goodnight here." She touched his arm. "Thanks for dinner." Not bothering to wait for a response, Jada hurried out of the car and didn't look back as she made her way up the walkway to the house.

"Wow, you're home early," Christina said from the stairs when Jada walked in and closed the door. "What happen with Mr. Money Bags? By the looks of him, he seemed to fit your usual requirements: tall, dark, and perfect white teeth. And I see you arrived home hair intact and no mud on your face."

"Ha, ha, ha, I see you have jokes." Jada passed Christina on the stairs. They turned the corner and walked toward Jada's room. "He fits some of my requirements, but he's a little too self-centered for my taste."

"Yeah, I guess two self-centered people aren't a good match." Sarcasm dripped from Christina's words. "If he's talking about himself all night, that means he didn't give you a chance to talk about yourself."

"Whatever." Jada had to admit Christina was right. Normally guys wanted to hear all about her and talk about how good she looked. She had never thought much of it, but wondered if some of her dates felt like she did tonight.

"You didn't tell me much about your date with Zack Anderson. Do you think you'll go out with him again?"

"Ha! Not if I have to dig in dirt."

"What made him think you'd be up to something like that? He had to know by looking at you that you don't do much manual labor – except for at work. And even that's questionable."

Jada shot her cousin an evil glare. Even if she were

telling the truth, Jada didn't appreciate the dig. She stepped into the walk-in closet and slipped out of her dress, replacing the garment with a satin robe that stopped at her knees. Exiting the closet, she thought about the little white lie she'd told Zack while they'd danced, the white lie that had come back to bite her in the butt. "I might have led him to believe that I do volunteer work and enjoy the outdoors."

Christina stared at her for a moment and then burst out laughing. "Why in the world would you say something like that? If it weren't for your shopping addiction, you wouldn't even go to work. And don't get me started on how gramma has to practically beg you to help in her garden. Maybe I need to set Zack straight about you."

"Nope. You stay away from him."

"So are you planning to see him again?"

Jada zoned in on the small hamper holding her dirty clothes. Zack wasn't the type of man she'd normally be attracted to, but she had to admit she'd enjoyed spending time with him. She typically gravitated to the CEOs, and wealthy entrepreneurs, but after dating Marcus, she now wondered if she could enjoy a rich life without passion.

Plopping down on the bed next to Christina, she said, "To answer your question, I'm not sure … but maybe."

CHAPTER SEVEN

Zack embraced the tranquility surrounding him, as well as the beautiful woman in his arms. Peace settled in his soul, and he exhaled a long sigh, glad he was able to convince Jada to go out again.

She relaxed against him as they lounged on a blanket, staring out over the water. They had arrived at the nature preserve a half an hour before the sun rose, and Zack couldn't ever remember experiencing such a peaceful moment with anyone before.

"Thank you for bringing me here." Jada glanced over her shoulder, the back of her head brushing against his chest. "This is breathtaking," she said of the sun glowing over the water. I've lived here all my life and never knew of a place to come where I could see an actual sunrise. And just think, yesterday I almost said no thank you once you mentioned picking me up at four-thirty this morning."

Zack laughed. "Well, I'm glad you didn't turn me down. I like having you here with me."

Hiking up the winding trails along the ridge often helped Zack clear his head while getting in a workout. The trip today was different, giving him an opportunity to share something special with Jada. Sure they had talked a number of times over the last two weeks, but being with her was so much more rewarding than a simple telephone call.

"Let me see your palm?" She lifted her left hand to him. "It still looks a little red. Does it hurt?"

"It stings a little, but I'll live. If I had been paying attention, I wouldn't have tripped over the roots of that tree." She shook her head and smiled, her whole face lighting up. "I think I might've still been half asleep. I guess you can probably tell that I'm not a morning person."

He linked his fingers with hers and stared at their joined hands, her brown skin a stark contrast next to his pale skin. He hadn't dated a black woman since college but learned early on that where it mattered, most women were the same.

Zack released her hand and pushed a loose strand of hair out of her face, slipping the silky lock behind her ear. She felt right in his arms. Actually, the whole morning felt right, as if they were right where they were supposed to be.

"I guess fall is finally here," she said, snuggling closer to him. "When October first rolled around, and we still had seventy degree weather, I started to believe there was something to this global warming thing."

Zack nodded, his chin brushing against the softness of her hair. "Yeah, you're right. It has been warmer than usual this time of year. Personally, I'm glad it's finally cooling off. When I'm on the field with all of my gear on, it's as if the temperature is at least twenty degrees hotter."

"You must be naturally hot-blooded. You're not wearing a jacket while I have on a jacket and a sweater."

They talked and laughed for a few minutes more. This connection is what Zack had been missing, what he'd been yearning. A woman who could share in some of the activities he enjoyed without complaining every couple of minutes that they didn't want to get dirty, or they were tired, or they were afraid of bugs.

When Jada shivered again, despite his arm being around

her, he knew it was time to pack everything up and leave. He wasn't ready to end their time together, but considering how long it took them to get there, it was probably a good idea to start heading back.

"Are you ready to go?" He kissed Jada on the cheek, her hair tickling his nose. Both his arms wrapped around her as she sat between his legs, her back to his chest.

"I'm not ready, but I guess we probably should head out." She turned slightly in his arms, her lips mere inches from his. He stared into her sexy brown eyes and then his gaze dropped to her tempting mouth. He looked up to find her still staring at him, and a sensuous light passed between them. They wanted the same thing.

Zack moved his body to the right slightly, his fingers caressing her cheek. Without saying a word, he lowered his head and their lips touched. The kiss started slow and exploratory, but quickly spiraled out of control. Jada moaned and pulled away from him slightly. Turning on her knees, she faced him and wrapped her arms around his neck, reclaiming his lips. It was his turn to moan when she increased the pressure of their kiss. He was shocked at her eager response, loving her boldness as their tongues tangled to a sensuous tune.

Zack lowered her to the blanket, laying her on her back without breaking contact. He wanted her like a moth wanted light. They'd talked periodically over the last couple of weeks and his desire for her had multiplied since the last time he'd seen her.

Lying next to her, he cradled her head in the crook of his arm, while his other hand slid under her sweater, stopping at the lace covering her firm breast. "Ah baby," he mumbled against her lips, his control slipping. Every night, visions of her crept into his mind, dominated his dreams and left him frustrated when he'd wake up to find her not there. Right now, he would give anything to have her. All of her.

Reveling in the softness of her body against his, Zack slid

on top of her, careful to support his weight. His hand still between their bodies, his fingers tweaking her erect nipple through the laced bra. His shaft throbbed behind his zipper. No doubt she felt the effect she was having on him against her thigh. Everything about Jada turned him on. From that sassy wit and curvy body to the erotic whimpers slipping through her soft, sensual lips.

He lowered his hand to her flat stomach and lifted his head slightly. "I know this is a fine time to ask, but are you dating anyone … exclusively?"

Her eyes lowered, and she licked her lips before her gaze met his again. "No," she mumbled, her voice raspy.

"Good."

"Are you?" He hesitated, and she leaned away and narrowed her eyes at him. If only she knew how much he cared about her, how much he craved her. She would've understood what a crazy question that was.

"I am now." His voice gruff with desire as he reclaimed her lips with an urgency he had never felt before, needing her to feel what he felt in his heart. He wanted her more than he had ever wanted anyone, but it was too soon. He wanted forever and didn't intend on screwing up whatever was developing between them by moving too fast.

Jada's moans stoked the flames burning inside of him. But if he didn't stop soon, he wouldn't be able to stop, and he didn't want their first time to be outside on the hard ground.

He raised up on his elbows and stared down at her. "You are so damn beautiful," he mumbled hoarsely, caressing her cheek.

"I could say the same thing about you." She wiped lipstick from his mouth with the pad of her thumb, her finger lingering longer than necessary.

"I guess we should go." He raised up and helped her into a sitting position.

"You mentioned that we're going back down the trail a

different way."

He nodded. "Yeah, we'll walk along the water's edge for a ways and then go down a back way to the truck." He stood, grasped her hand, and pulled her up. "It's picturesque and it'll give you a chance to see different scenery than what we did coming up here."

"I can't imagine it being any more beautiful than this area." She walked to the edge of the water as Zack cleaned up the extra food from their picnic, loading it into the backpack that he had carried. Picking up the used napkins, paper plates and cups, he shoved them into a small trash bag he had thought to bring.

Zack glanced over to where Jada stood. Everything about the time he'd been spending with her felt different than it had with Leslie. They both were very beautiful women, but he couldn't believe how fast he had taken to Jada. His mother often said that when its right, its right. He never knew exactly what *it* was, but he had a feeling Jada was right for him.

***

Jada stood next to the water, her hands shoved into the pockets of her Burberry jacket. They had been at the reserve for hours, and she wished they could stay forever. She glanced back at Zack, who was still cleaning up. Returning her attention to the water, her fingertips lightly touching her lips, still felt warm from his kiss. *Damn he can kiss, but what am I doing?* Her mind relived the velvet warmth of his mouth. If she weren't careful, Zack could become an addiction she couldn't break. Hooking up with a man because of his wealth and companionship was one thing, but she couldn't risk falling for someone who had the ability to break her heart.

A ripple in the water caught her attention.

What the heck? Is that a fish? She stepped closer, not caring that Christina's boots were getting wet.

"Be careful Jada, those rocks can get a little slippery,"

Zack called out from their picnic spot.

"Okay." She slowly treaded through the shallow, clear water noticing moss, colorful pebbles, and algae, but no fish. Why she was so determined to see a fish up close was a mystery to her considering she didn't really like the slippery little creatures.

A frustrated growl rumbled in her throat as she swatted at a bug flying too close to her face. *That's another reason I don't like being outside. Stupid insects.*

Another ripple in the water a few feet out grabbed her attention again.

"Ready to go?" Zack asked.

Jada glanced over her shoulder at him, surprised at just how far she had walked out.

"Yep, I'm ready." She turned to retrace her steps, but whipped her head back around when she heard a soft splash. "Whoa!" Her foot slipped, and she tried desperately to steady herself. Her arms flailed as she wobbled back and forth.

"Jada!" Zack yelled. Heavy footsteps pounded through the crunching leaves covering the ground. "Jada!" Before she could look at him, her feet slid from beneath her.

"Aarrggghh!" Her earsplitting scream pierced the quietness of their surroundings. It was as if she were falling in slow motion. Her arms flopped around, and her heart pounded wildly in her chest. All thoughts flew from her mind. She squeezed her eyes shut, landing with a splash in the cold shallow water.

"*Ohmigod! Ohmigod*!" She splashed around, arms flailing, legs kicking, water flying everywhere. She screamed again, when she tried to stand, only to slip back down, frustrated by her clumsiness.

"Jada." She startled, not noticing that Zack had come up behind her. "Are you okay?" He grabbed her underneath her armpits and lifted her into a standing position.

"Yeah." Her unsteady legs barely held her up as she

gripped his arm tightly. "You were right. It is slippery out here." She tried to make light of the situation, hoping he didn't think she was a total klutz.

"Are you sure you're okay? You're not hurt, are you?"

She slowly released the death grip on his arm. "Only my pride." She took a deep breath in and slowly let it out forcing her heart to reclaim its steady beat. Soaking wet from the top of her head to the soles of her feet, if she didn't get out of the water and those clothes soon, she was guaranteed to catch a cold. Or worse, die from hyperthermia.

Still sliding on the rocks, unable to maintain her balance, Jada grabbed hold of Zack's arm again. How was it that he was able to stand next to her without sliding around the way she was? Sure, he might've had an extra seventy-five to a hundred pounds on her, but still…

"Come on let's get you out of this wat—"

"Aarrggghh!" Jada screamed when she lost her footing. Again, her arms flailed, her legs kicked, unable to get her balance despite Zack's efforts to get a grip on her jacket.

"Jada stop … oh sh…!" Zack's feet slipped from beneath him, when she grabbed hold of the tail of his flannel shirt on her way down. She ducked, hoping he wouldn't fall on her, but he landed on the side of her with a huge splash and curse words flying out of his mouth.

"Ohmigod! Are you okay?" Jada splashed around and frantically brushed her hair out of her face to glance over her shoulder at him. Their eyes met …seconds passed … and they burst out laughing.

"Are you okay?" she asked between giggles that turned into a full-blown laugh, unable to help herself. She could only imagine what they must look like flopping around like ducks in ankle deep water. Still laughing she said, "I … am … so sorry."

"Un…freakin…believable," Zack said shaking his head, a smile plastered on his face. "First you almost give me a heart attack, *twice*, and then you try to kill me." He slicked his wet hair back away from his forehead. "What am I going to do with you?"

Jada glanced down, finding it hard to believe she was sitting in water fully clothed. "Well, for starters you can help me up."

"Alright, but this time I'm carrying you. Clearly you can't walk on rocks." He stood slowly, getting his footing and then bent down and lifted her out of the water.

Jada wrapped her arms around his neck tightly. "Please don't drop me."

"Sweetheart, you're a lightweight. I'm not going to drop you, but can you loosen your grip? I can't breathe."

"Oh." Jada grinned and relaxed her arms. "Sor … ry." A chill roared through her body, and her teeth clattered. Shivering, she nestled against Zack, getting colder by the minute.

"I should have some extra clothes in the truck for us to change into." Zack set her on her feet once they were back on solid ground. Jada rubbed her hands up and down her arms, bouncing from one foot to the other until Zack snatched off the blanket attached to his backpack. "Here, this might help a little." He wrapped the fleece material around her shoulders and pulled her close.

Still shivering, she closed her eyes, loving the feel of his arms around her, trying to warm her up despite the fact they both were soaking wet. He leaned down and his mouth covered hers in a sweet tender kiss, and heat spread through her body. Not enough warmth to make her forget she was standing in wet clothes and boots, but enough to make her sex clench with need. Zack took his time, licking, teasing, making love to her mouth, and leaving her wanting so much more.

"We better get going." He gave her one last peck on her lips before picking up the backpack and slipping his arms through the straps. "Instead of the scenic route, we'll take the shortest trail."

Bouncing around, Jada nodded. "Good idea." Glancing back at the water, she shook her head. She prided herself on being sophisticated. The type of woman a man would love to have on his arm. But on each date with him, she came out looking like a total goof.

"Zack, I'm sorry," Jada said as they moved toward the walking trail.

He slowed and looked down at her, a frown marring his handsome face. "Sorry for what?"

"For this." She glanced down at their clothes. "All of this. You planned such a nice picnic date, and I ruined it. I am so sorry."

"Sweetheart, you have no reason to be sorry. I'm the one who should be apologizing. I should have made sure I stayed close to you, especially knowing how slippery those rocks can get." He squeezed her hand. "I'm just glad you're not hurt."

"Yeah, me too. But I have a feeling I'm going to remember this moment every time I try sit down, at least for the next few days."

He released her hand and gently palmed her butt as if he were holding a football, and pulled her against his hard body. "Well, if you need me to massage a certain part of your anatomy," he said, his voice deep and sensual, sent a ripple of excitement through her veins, "just say the word, and I'm there."

Jada gulped and stared into his sexy eyes. "Okay," she croaked, unable to form any other words. This man had the power to short circuit any common sense she had, and Jada could feel herself falling for him. Falling hard.

CHAPTER EIGHT

"So what gives? You haven't gone out on the town in a couple of weeks, which has to be a first," CJ said strolling into the living room.

Jada lounged on the sofa, her feet on the coffee table as she flipped through television stations. She didn't know how people sat in front of the TV all day every day when there was nothing good on.

When she turned the channel to a football game, she stopped, hoping Cincinnati was playing. She didn't know much about football, but thanks to her cousin Nick, she knew more now that she and Zack were seeing each other.

"Ahh, so that's it."

"What's it?" Jada glanced at Christina when she sat next to her. "And if you start throwing out some of your big, stupid words, I'm going to shove this remote down your throat." She held the television remote next to CJ's face, daring her.

"Oh stop." Christina swatted Jada's hand away. "I don't do the words anymore. It wasn't as much fun as I thought it would be. Most of the people I talk to are you and our cousins. Kinda like talking to a brick wall."

"Whatever." Jada grinned. She had to give her cousin credit for trying to build her vocabulary, especially considering the type of networking she had to do in her secret life. The part of her life that the rest of the family didn't know existed.

Jada turned her attention to the television. The Cincinnati Cougars weren't playing, but according to the sports announcer, their game was up next.

"Since you're watching football, does that mean that you and Zack are getting serious?"

"I'm watching football because there's nothing else on." Jada, not sure why, hadn't told her cousin that she and Zack were exclusive. Maybe because what she felt for him still made her a little nervous.

"Yeah, right. You're watching football because there is nothing else on? Tell it to someone who doesn't know you." Christina moved around trying to get comfortable on the sofa. "I guess since the Cougars have had away games the last two weeks, you've had to settle for trying to get a glimpse of Zack during the game on TV, huh?"

Jada couldn't ever remember missing someone as much as she missed Zack. *So much for protecting my heart.* Memories of a time where she allowed herself to get emotionally attached to a man came flooding into her mind. *Dion Greely.* The man she'd met and fallen in love with three years ago, the first and only man to break her heart. Jada made the mistake of thinking that eating at fancy restaurants, being whisked away on weekend trips, and receiving expensive gifts meant he loved her. That was a lesson learned quickly, and she vowed never again. Finding out he was married with a child wasn't as easy to get over. The knowledge nearly destroyed her emotionally. Dion had made it clear that even if he weren't already married, he'd never be able to marry someone who didn't have anything to bring to the table besides a pretty face and a tight body.

"You know, I'm a little shocked by your behavior,"

Christina said, breaking into Jada's thoughts. "Over the past month, you've complained about the less than glamourous dates that Zack has taken you on, yet you're still interested in him. So how do you explain that?"

Jada couldn't explain her desire to be with him. Yet, she had determined early on that Zack was nothing like Dion. Zack had morals, compassion, and treated her special. Most importantly, he wasn't married. However, after the third date with him, when he had taken her to a movie and then to a hotdog joint afterwards, she had vowed that that would be the last date with him. Then she couldn't for the life of her understand why she'd agreed to go fishing with him three days later, only to return home smelling like a swamp. She had knocked over the fish bucket and water splashed on her. That should have been the last straw. Yet here she was, watching football, hoping to get a glimpse of him because she hadn't seen him in a few days. The last time was over an early morning breakfast before she reported to work and he went to football practice.

"I like him. I *really* like him," Jada finally responded.

"I like Zack too. He doesn't seem as shallow as your other boy-toys. But why do *you* like him? He doesn't fit your required characteristics, except for being cute and rich. He doesn't take you to overpriced restaurants. He hasn't bought you any expensive gifts unless you count the purple tools and drill," she laughed, "and he doesn't come across like a pompous jackass. So why are you even bothering with him?"

"I'm not totally sure," Jada mumbled. "I think it's the way he makes me laugh and the way he makes me feel." She sat up and turned to Christina. "I also appreciate how real he is. He clearly is not trying to impress me." They both laughed. "He's attentive. Not in a – he's trying to get into my panties way, but in a he is truly trying to get to know me way. Not the shallow me," she said sheepishly, "but the real me. The me who has feelings. The me who loves attention and the me who wants to be happy."

"So what are you going to do about Zack's lack of dating savvy?" CJ removed the scrunchy from around her wrist and pulled her curly hair out of her face and up into a ponytail. "Maybe he's just cheap."

Jada fell back against the sofa. "Nah I don't think that's it. He gives tons of money to charities. He lives in Indian Hill not too far from Gramma and Grampa, and he has a place near the stadium, as well as a home in California. Don't get me started on all of the cars he owns. So, I don't think he's cheap. I think he just has a different idea of what fun is."

"Well, he must be doing something right if he has you sitting by the phone and watching football." Jada rolled her eyes and didn't bother responding. "Okay, but seriously, why do you think he can't plan better dates?"

"I don't have a clue. Outside of coming right out and telling him that I hate *all* outdoor activities, that hotdogs make me gag, and that I'm looking to marry rich so that I can quit my construction job, I'm not sure what to do."

"Why don't you show him?" Christina put her feet on the floor and sat up.

Jada looked at her cousin sideways. "Show him what?"

"Show him how you like to be treated. Insist that he get dressed up. *You* take him to a fine dining establishment, to the theater, and do all the other crap you like doing." Her cousin stood and stretched her arms above her head, her short T-shirt rising up showing off light brown skin and flat abs. "If he doesn't catch a hint then, you might want to cut your losses and move on to your next victim."

Jada smiled, ideas for an exciting evening running rampant through her mind. "I can't believe I'm going to say this, but you might be on to something. I'll plan a nice romantic evening for next weekend. Friday I'm working a half a day. After his team's workout, he's taking me 4-wheeling."

"Hmm, that sounds like fun. The last cruise I went on, I

had planned to go 4-wheeling on one of the excursions, but the outing was canceled. Since then, I haven't thought about going. Hopefully, you'll have a good time."

"I hope so too. I have barely survived his dates. If he wants to keep me, he's going to have to step up his game in regards to these dates."

"I'm sure he'll catch on … eventually. In the meantime, I definitely think you're going to have to teach him how you want to be treated."

The doorbell rang.

"I'll get it." Christina walked out of the living room and down the short hall to the front door. Minutes later, she came back carrying a box the size of a boot box. "A delivery for Ms. Jada Jenkins from Mr. Zachary Anderson." She waved a small envelope. "It looks like your man sent you a gift. Maybe he's already caught a hint. The box is from Bloomingdales."

Jada jumped up from the sofa, excitement streaming through her veins. "Oh my goodness!" He'd sent her a case of Acqua Di Gioia, her favorite perfume a month ago and had been sending flowers for the last couple of weeks. "I can't imagine what's in this box, but I hope it's the Marc Jacob's boots that I mentioned to him when we went out to lunch last weekend."

"How would he know which ones to get?"

Jada twisted her lips in a grin. "Well, while we were waiting for our food, I happen to have a magazine with the boots in it, and I might've shown them to him."

Christina shook her head and grinned. "Of course you did."

Jada grabbed a pair of scissors from the drawer near the built-in bookshelf and hurried back to the sofa. Christina stood nearby.

"Oh please, please, please be the Marc…" Her voice trailed off when she made it through the first box and pulled out a smaller boot box with Timberland printed across the top. "What the heck?" She opened the box and pulled out a pair of wheat color suede-like boots that resembled her steel-toe boots.

Christina fell to her knees. Holding her stomach, she rolled around on the floor laughing. When her cousin pounded the floor with her hand, unable to catch her breath, Jada admitted it might've been a little funny, but it wasn't that funny.

Zack cannot be this clueless.

When she finally calmed herself, her cousin swiped the back of her hand across her eyes to wipe the moisture from them. "As I've said before, I like Zack. If nothing else, he's great comic relief." Still on the floor, she sat with her back against the sofa and grabbed one of the Timberland boots, holding it out in front of her. "What does the card say?"

Disappointed, Jada reluctantly pulled the notecard from the envelope.

"*Hey sweetheart, I can't wait to see you in the morning. Thought you might need these for when we go 4-wheeling. I hope you like them. Until tomorrow. Zack.*"

"Well, at least he got the size right."

"Yeah, whatever. He just better hope I enjoy 4-wheeling. Otherwise, I'm done."

***

"That's it!" Jada screamed, her arms flailing around, anger marring her muddy face. "Do not call me. Do not come by my job. Do not send me gi…gifts. Lose my damn number!" Her finger stabbed the air, punctuating each one of her words. "Look at my clothes! And my hair," she sobbed.

Stunned, Zack could only stare at her. They'd gone 4-wheeling, and things were going well until they hopped on one of the most challenging trails full of potholes and mud. How was he to know that she would lose control and hit a mud puddle? Besides, who wore a white jacket when they knew they were going 4-wheeling?

"Don't you think you're over reacting?" Zack folded his

arms across his chest. "They're just clothes, Jada. Hell, I'll be glad to replace the whole outfit." A clump of mud from a few strands of wayward hair sticking out from under her helmet, fell to the ground. "And your hair can be washed."

"You don't get it do you?" She slowly approached him, the vein in her forehead protruding, her jaw and fists clenched. Now he was the one who was taking slow steps back. Anger leaked from every pore in her body. "All you've been thinking about is yourself with these stupid dates! We have gone hiking, fishing, hung out in your mechanic's garage, played around in dirt and now this – driving through mud!" Her voice grew louder with each word. "What woman in her right mind would enjoy this?"

"Well, damn, Jada!" He dropped his arms to his sides and yelled back. "You never, not once, said you didn't like the activities I planned!" His arms flailed around; annoyance quickly turning into anger. "Hell, if you were having such a rotten time, why didn't you say something? You had plenty of opportunities! How in the heck was I supposed to know that you weren't enjoying yourself? I thought—"

"You thought what?" She pointed her finger at him, barely missing his face. "That just because I work in construction that I don't like the finer things in life? That I don't like to get dressed up and go to the theater, a concert, or hell a five-star restaurant. While you were planning all of these activities, did you even think of me once? Did you ever ask yourself, *I wonder what Jada would enjoy doing*?"

"Hold up. Wait!" Zack braced his index fingers against his temples, closed his eyes, and tried to wrap his brain around all that she was saying. Had he missed some signs? He opened his eyes and glared at her. "Let me make sure I have this right. You're mad at me because I suggested that we do some outdoor activities. Mind you, this is after *you* told me you were a go-with-the-flow kind of girl who loves the outdoors. So now you're telling me that that's not the case? So what the hell was that conversation on the dance floor all about?"

Silence fell between them, both their chests heaving. Jada wiped at the mud that covered her face, only making it worse.

"It's time I was honest with you, Zack." She leaned against the truck. The hairs on the back of Zack's neck stood at attention as trepidation rose through his body and lodged in his chest. Thoughts of Leslie and the way she had lied and used him immediately came to the forefront of his mind.

Jada let out a loud breath and removed the helmet from her head, dropping it to the ground. She bent over slightly, hands perched on her thighs, her head hung low. Thinking that she was going to be sick, Zack inched toward her but stopped when she lifted her head.

"I hate getting my hands dirty." She pushed hair away from her face and shivered when she lowered her hand and saw more mud caked under her French manicure. "I don't like animals, not even goldfish, and the day I volunteered at the farm was the first time I'd done any volunteering since girl's scouts." She glanced down at her clothes. Zack thought she was going to burst into tears.

Why hadn't she said something sooner? Most importantly, why had she lied about being an outdoorsy person?

Facing the truck, Jada folded her arms against the vehicle and rested her forehead on her arms. Eventually, she peeked back at him. "I like you ... God, I like you so much, Zack, but by now I thought you'd figure out the real me. Despite being a sheet metal worker, I'm a woman who enjoys ... woman things. I get my hair and nails done at *least* once a week because I like to look good at *all* times. I only wear designer clothes, even to work, because I think it's important to always look your best. I love my family more than anything in the world, and I enjoy working at the family business. But to be honest, I work there to support my shopping addiction." She exhaled loudly, tears rolling down her face. "I'm clearly not the woman for you and I'm sorry for leading you to think that I am."

Zack studied her. Disappointment descended on him like a two-ton boulder. He had opened his heart to yet another woman only to have her lie to him too, and over something so trivial. Had she lied about her feelings for him? Was their time together, their laughs and conversations all a lie? He could deal with a lot of things, but even if he did love her, he couldn't deal with a liar.

"Zack, I'm so sorry. I should've been upfront with you from the beginning."

"Why weren't you?"

She hesitated. "Because—"

"No. You know what? Don't bother." He shook his head and walked past her and opened the passenger side door, not caring that the interior was going to be full of mud. "Jada, I don't like games and I can't handle any more lies, especially not from you." From someone, he could see spending the rest of his life with, from someone he had fallen in love with.

"Zack please let me explain."

"I'll take you home and you'll never have to see me again."

CHAPTER NINE

Five days later and Zack still hadn't gotten Jada out of his system. He hadn't called her, and she hadn't called him. Not that he expected her to. His only regret, well his main regret, was not giving her the opportunity to tell him why she had lied in the first place.

"You want another beer?" Craig, who was sitting on the bar stool next to him asked.

"I'm good thanks." Craig had invited him to have a drink at their favorite downtown bar and grill. For the past thirty minutes, they had been hanging out talking while Zack signed a few autographs for fans in between conversations.

Craig sipped his rum and coke. "A few weeks ago, you were saying that Jada was the one. That she was special and filled a void in your life that you had been trying to fill for years. Now you find out she exaggerated the truth, and you've kicked her to the curb. Do you think that's fair?"

"Zack Anderson!" A man standing a few feet away called out. "Great game Sunday."

"Thanks."

"Can I get your autograph?"

Zack absently signed the napkin that the guy handed him.

He thought back on his and Jada's various dates and the number of hours they had spent talking on the telephone. He'd gotten to know her. There were similarities between her and his ex, but unlike with Leslie, he had experienced Jada's sweetness, kindness, and her compassion.

Jada is the one. But I can't get pass the lie.

"Last one," Zack said signing yet another napkin handed to him by a fan.

"You seem to be handling all the attention you've been getting better than you used to."

"Some days are better than others." There was a time when Craig and Donny refused to go out in public with him, especially during football season, thanks to the number of fans who approached Zack wanting to take a picture with him or get his autograph. "Okay, let's get back to our conversation. Are you saying that I should overlook the fact that Jada lied? Who knows what else she lied about?" He lowered his voice as the bar area grew crowded. "If it were Toni, you're saying that you would overlook the deceit."

Craig chuckled. "You do remember the hell Toni put me through don't you?" They both laughed though there was a time when Toni and Craig's issues weren't a laughing matter. Toni was always getting herself into jams, some more serious than others. Yet, Craig never gave up on her. "Zack, I know you have trust issues, and your last relationship didn't help, but Jada is not Leslie. Yes, she has expensive taste and wants to live a life of luxury, but she's good people. She talks a tough game, but she wouldn't intentionally hurt anyone, especially not you. Do you love her?"

Whew. Zack turned back to the bar, wrapping his hands around his cold bottle of beer. *Do you love her?* Yeah, he loved her.

He lifted his head and stared into the mirror behind the bar. As if thinking about Jada conjured her up, she walked in with her cousins. He glanced over his shoulder, and his stomach knotted with desire.

Damn, she looks good. The pink, form-fitting sweater showed off her perky breasts, and a wide black belt emphasized her slender waist. Zack's gaze traveled lower. Seeing how the tight black jeans hugged her round butt and shapely thighs sent blood rushing from his head down to another part of his anatomy. Part of him wanted to go to her, but instead he admired her from afar, wishing he could hold her in his arms again.

Toni broke away from the group and made a beeline for the bar, which is when Jada's gaze met his. Her eyes grew large, and her mouth gaped open. They didn't break eye contact until one of her cousins nudged her and pointed to an empty booth.

"Here's my baby." Craig stood and watched Toni's approach.

"Why do I feel like I've been set up?" Zack mumbled.

Craig gripped Zack's shoulder. "Because you have. Man, talk to her and see if you can't make things right between you two."

"Hey, Baby." Toni kissed Craig on the lips before turning her attention to Zack and shoved him in the arm. "The only reason I agreed to help with this little match-making scheme is because I think you're good for my cousin. Hurt her," her finger wagged in his face, "and you'll have to deal with me."

Zack smiled, trying hard to hold back a laugh. Toni stood about two inches shorter than Jada and the thought of her pint-sized self, causing any real damage, was comical.

Craig nodded his head toward the booth, where Jada and her cousins sat. "You need to make the first move. Talk to her. Admit to your role in all of this."

Zack turned back to the bar and finished off his beer. In all of his efforts to get to know Jada and spend time with a woman who claimed to enjoy the outdoors as much as him, he failed to acknowledge the other side of her. The more feminine side. The girly girl side that looked damn good in everything she wore and always smelled like a bouquet of roses. The side that turned him on with very little effort.

Talk about selfish. Zack could kick himself. Jada had been such a trooper with the activities that he had planned. Yet, he hadn't thought about doing some of the things that women enjoyed. Hadn't even asked for her input as it related to their dates. He shook his head. Yeah, he needed to make this right and hoped it wasn't too late.

***

"Are you all right, Cuz?" Peyton put her arm around Jada's shoulder. "You've been eyeing Zack since we sat down. Why don't you just go over and say hi."

Jada shrugged Peyton's arm away. "Were all of you in on this? Tricking me to come here so that I could run into him?" The moment her gaze met Zack's, heat rose to her cheeks. Knowing that he was angry with her didn't squash the lust pulsing through her veins at the sight of seeing him across the room. She had hurt him. The ache in her heart made her want to hightail it out of the bar. She would never forget the pain in his eyes when he dropped her off at home after their 4-wheeling adventure.

"For the record, we didn't know he would be here, but it doesn't matter now. Your man is on his way over," CJ whispered.

Jada's pulse hammered in her chest when Zack stopped at their table. *God, he looks good.* She licked her lips at the way his navy blue, long-sleeved T-shirt hugged his wide chest and muscular arms. The dark jeans molded to his legs that went on forever were absolutely drool worthy. By the appreciative glances directed at him from other women in the room, she wasn't the only one impressed with what she saw.

"Hello ladies." Zack's deep, baritone voice reverberated through Jada's body, and it took everything she had not to leap from the table and jump into his arms. She held back a groan. His presence alone made her body hum.

I have it bad. I have it real bad.

"Hey, world's greatest running back, it's good seeing you again," MJ said.

"Hi Zack," Peyton and Christina said in unison.

"Jada, can I speak to you for a minute?"

Jada nodded afraid any words she spoke would sound like gibberish. Zack offered her his hand, and she grabbed hold, allowing him to help her stand. An electric charge shot up her arm, and a tremor gripped her body. His touch still had the ability to make her weak in the knees. He held onto her hand as he guided her outside and didn't release her until they were several feet away from the entrance.

"Now that I have you out here, I'm not sure what to say." He shoved his hands into his front pockets.

"Well, just so that you know, I had nothing to do with all of this – us meeting up here. I told you my family was nosy, and I think they roped poor Craig into playing along."

Zack laughed. The rich timbre of the sound made her warm all over. It had been a long time since a man brought her happiness, but with Zack, he had already proven that he also had the power to break her heart too.

"Don't feel too sorry for Craig. I just found out he was the mastermind behind this plan." Zack's dimples made an appearance, weakening Jada's restraint. She so wanted to wrap her arms around his neck and taste his sweet lips.

He glanced down at his blue hiking boots and kicked a rock with his foot. "I have to say," he met her gaze, "I'm glad they butted in. Otherwise, I don't know if I would've had enough sense to contact you and tell you that I'm sorry."

Jada leaned back and frowned. "*You're* sorry? What do you have to be sorry about? I'm the one who wasn't completely honest with you." She toyed with her large, sparkly belt buckle trying to find the words to tell him how she felt. "I should have been straight with you, Zack."

He grabbed hold of her hand, stopping her from fidgeting. "I have to ask, why did you tell me that you do volunteer work and enjoyed the outdoors if those things aren't what you enjoy doing?"

She started to pull away, but he held her tight, halting her retreat.

"I guess I wanted to impress you." She lowered her lashes.

"Jada?" He tugged on her hand.

"Huh? Oh sorry." She paused, debating on what to say to him. "You … you were so fascinated that I worked in construction. And when you mentioned you enjoyed the outdoors and volunteering," she gave a slight shrug, "I just went along with you. I guess I got carried away. I never expected I'd have to prove my love of those things. A date for me is an opportunity to wear a beautiful dress, enjoy a gourmet meal and an aged bottle of Merlot. And If I'm lucky an engaging conversation."

He caressed her cheek and goose bumps skittered up and down her arms. "Why didn't you tell me sooner that you hated that stuff?"

"You made our adventures fun. Besides, I wanted to be near you. I wanted to get to know you better, even if it meant ruining my clothes and wearing those ugly hiking boots."

Zack grinned. "I take it you weren't feeling the footwear."

Jada fought a smile, and she shook her head. "They remind me too much of my steel-toe work boots."

Framing her face with his large hands, Zack lowered his forehead to hers. He didn't speak right away, and they stood that way for the longest, staring into each other's eyes.

"I messed up. I allowed my trust issues to get in the way, without giving you a chance to explain. I'm also a jerk for not realizing sooner how selfish I was being."

"Zack, this was not your fault."

"Yeah, some of it was, but I'm asking you to give me one more chance to prove I'm not the bonehead that you probably think I am. Sweetheart, I'm crazy about you. I want to show you just how much you mean to me. Have dinner with me at my place tomorrow night."

His lips touched hers, before she had a chance to respond, and liquid heat shot through her body. Jada had thought that the last time she saw him would be the last time she saw him. His kiss radiated heat throughout her body, setting fire to every nerve ending along its way. She loved him. Loved him more than she ever thought possible.

I am in so much trouble.

CHAPTER TEN

"Dinner was delicious." Jada wiped her mouth and pushed away from the small, round table. "I can't believe you went through all of this trouble." Her gaze roamed around the intimate space of his sunroom and the wall-to-wall windows that overlooked his back yard. Lights hung from the multi-level deck, as well as every tree and a gazebo off in the distance, making the yard look like a winter wonderland without the snow. Even the in-ground pool, which was covered, had built in lights around its perimeter, shining brightly. "This is the most romantic dinner I've ever had. The candles," she waved her arm around the room, "the wine, a meal befitting of a five-star restaurant, and great conversation – thank you. Everything was amazing."

Zack scooted his chair closer, and his hand caressed the back of her neck. Her eyes drifted shut. If he was trying to seduce her, it was working. He had been touching her with such gentleness all night, and Jada knew that if he kept up the sweet torture, she was going to embarrass herself by begging him to take her right then, and there.

"I have a few more surprises for you tonight," he whispered close to her ear, placing a soft kiss on her neck.

A moan rose to her throat. Her eyelids fluttered, and she stared into his dreamy blue eyes, lost in their tenderness. Her heart did cartwheels inside her chest at his nearness, his lips only inches from hers.

"Zack you're killing me here," she said breathlessly, her body throbbing with need.

He grinned and stood, pulling her to her feet. His silence only amplified the desire flowing through her body, sending her heart rate to an immeasurable level. She watched as he blew out candles around the room, her gaze following every move of his tall, muscular body. The man oozed sex appeal, and Jada had to pinch herself to make sure the evening wasn't a dream.

Her temperature rose with each step he took toward her. So much time had passed since she allowed a man near her heart. Yet Zack had somehow penetrated the security that she had placed around it.

He stopped in front of her, and his hands eased around her waist pulling her against his hard body. Jada knew at that moment that Zack could ask anything of her, and she would do it. Lips so soft touched hers, and it felt as if that was the first time she had ever been kissed. A quivering stomach, sweaty palms and weak knees, all made her powerless in his arms.

Oh, this man…

He nipped her top lip, and then her lower one. His tongue traced her lips before sliding in and claiming her mouth. His kiss sang through her veins and her insides turned to mush. Peace filled her soul. *Oh, how I love this man.* Sooner than she wanted him to, he lifted his head and stared into her eyes.

"I know we have moved past what happened the other day, but going forward, I need you to tell me when you don't like something. You never have to settle for less than you want when you're with me. Understood?"

She nodded, still staring into his eyes.

"I plan to prove to you just how special you are to me, and I plan to start now. Let me show you something."

"Zack, you don't have to do anything else for me. I'm just glad to be here with you." He squeezed her hand without responding. They walked through the kitchen that would be any cook's dream space and headed to the spiral staircase. Light emitted from the impressive crystal chandelier over the stairs like stars sparkling in the night. Jada had been to Zack's house several times and each time she walked around in amazement of its magnificence.

Hand in hand, they made their way to the top landing and strolled down the extra-wide hallway, where four of the five bedrooms were located. Jada assumed they were going to Zack's bedroom, but when they stopped in front of a closed door, she wondered what he was up to. Before she could ask, he pushed the door open and escorted her in. Her breath caught in her lungs.

"Oh. My. God." Her hands hovered over her mouth, and tears welled up in her eyes. Seconds ticked by, as she stood stunned. "Who? When? How were you able to do all of this?"

Stepping into the room was like stepping into her own personal boutique with mirrors, racks of designer clothes, and tons of shoes and handbags perfectly displayed.

"I wasn't totally sure what you would like, so I figured I'd have a little bit of everything you could possibly need … or want, delivered. I had to do something to make up for all of the clothes that were ruined during our adventures."

"Zack," she said wistfully, her voice trailing off as she perused the items in the room. The racks of clothes lined the perimeter of the large space, while every possible accessory was displayed on tall tables, with drawers, in the center of the room.

"How did you do all of this?"

"I'll admit. I had some help. Okay, a lot of help." He moved slowly across the room and stopped at a table loaded with earrings and necklaces. "My mother is the queen of shopping and has a personal shopper on speed dial. So I connected her with your cousins Christina and Toni late last night. They gave her your sizes, your favorite designers and what you don't like," he shrugged, "and my mother took over from there."

Jada roamed around from one rack of clothes to the next awestruck. She didn't know much about his mother, except what he'd told her – that she was a little eccentric and flighty. Based on what was in the room, Jada couldn't wait to meet her. She would also have to thank her cousins. This was one time she was glad they knew her well.

There was something special about his attempt to make up for her ruined clothes and shoes. Each date they'd been on, he had made her feel as if she were the most important person in the world. Yet this felt different. He had gone out of his way to make things right and to please her as if she was much more than just someone he dated.

Jada shook her head in disbelief. Making her way to the far corner of the room, she saw the rows of boots in multiple colors and with various heel heights, but there was one pair that stood out. She picked up the boots and immediately recognized them as the pair of Marc Jacobs that she had been drooling over for the past couple of weeks.

Turning back to Zack, she held them up. Before she could say anything, he spoke.

"I hope those are the right ones. I was going by memory. You showed me an ad in that magazine the other week. I purchased them a few days later but hadn't decided when to give them to you. I figured this was as good of a time as any. The matching handbag should be in here somewhere too."

"You do know the real me," she whispered, holding the boots against her body. Tears rolled down her cheeks, and she didn't bother wiping them away. No one had ever done anything so thoughtful for her. She couldn't believe that Zack would go through so much trouble.

"Aw, sweetheart, don't cry." He took the boots out of her hands and laid them back on the shelf. "Of course I know you." He cradled her face with both of his hands, forcing her to meet his gaze. He wiped her tears away with the pad of his thumbs. "I know I goofed up these last couple of months, but don't think that I don't know you. I know that you are a passionate woman who loves her family. A woman who likes the finer things in life." His lips quirked as if trying to hide a smile. "And you're the woman that I love."

He claimed her lips, crushing her to him. She gave herself freely to the passion of his kiss, wanting so much more as spirals of ecstasy swirled through her body. Jada tried to ignore the building heat between her thighs, but it was impossible. Her thirst for Zack grew stronger than a bird's need to soar through the skies.

"Zack." She mumbled when his lips seared a path down her neck only stopping when he reached the collar of her Givenchy dress. Unable to form words, a whimper snuck out.

Zack returned to her mouth and covered her lips. He lowered the zipper, opening the front of her dress, and the soft material fell open. It had been a long time since she had made love to a man, but Jada had a feeling this experience with Zack would be like no other.

When he stepped back, his gaze pinned her in place. Those sexy blue eyes glittered with desire and had her squeezing her thighs together. He reached up and with both hands, pushed the dress from her shoulders, allowing the garment to tumble to the floor. Left with wearing only a teal bra and panty set that matched the discarded dress and black stilettos, Jada thought she was going to spontaneously combust. Heat spread from the top of her head to the soles of her feet. If he kept looking at her with longing in his eyes, she was going to have to take matters into her own hands.

"I knew you'd be beautiful under those fancy clothes you wear," a smile tipped the corner of his lips, "but you're absolutely breathtaking." The awe in his voice made her even more eager about what she knew was going to happen next. What she wanted to happen next.

Zack helped her out of her lacy undies. His skillful hands roamed slowly down the sides of her body until he reached the curve of her hip.

"I have to have you … now."

Stooping slightly, he gripped the back of her thighs and lifted her. Jada wrapped her legs around his waist and didn't have to ask where he was taking her as they left the room. She threw her arms around his head and held on, her bare breasts in his face.

"Mmm," Zack moaned, placing a lingering kiss on the inside of both of her breasts, the scruff on his jaw tickling her. He took his time carrying her across the hall and into the master bedroom. She trembled against the ball of giddiness that settled in the pit of her stomach, the prolonged anticipation almost unbearable. Jada had thought about this moment for a long time but didn't know when or if their relationship would make it to this level.

Zack didn't stop until he reached the bed. He loosened his grip, and her body slid down his – passion igniting within her, sending jolts of pleasure to the tips of her toes. Her feet touched the floor, and she watched as Zack removed his clothes. *Utter perfection*. That was the only way she could describe his body. There was no fat anywhere on the man. All Jada could do was stare. An elaborate tattoo started on the right side of his chest and snaked up and over his shoulder. The intricate details, with a multitude of colors and shapes, made it hard for her to believe someone used that type of talent on skin instead of canvas.

"Wow," she said, her voice filled with wonder. "This is remarkable." She traced some of the colorful swirls with her fingertip.

"No, sweetie, you're remarkable." Zack grabbed her hands, ceasing her exploration of his tattoo. He kissed the inside of one of her wrists and brought her arms up to his shoulder where she wrapped them around his neck. An involuntary shiver gripped her. Feeling Zack's hard body against hers, chest to chest, skin to skin, had her trembling with need. "I have wanted you from the moment I saw you walking down the aisle at Craig and Toni's wedding." Zack lifted her, gently easing her onto the bed, his strong, muscular body straddling her. "And finally..." His words trailed off as his lips connected with her neck, placing kisses along her collarbone and on down to her shoulder.

Jada drew in a breath against the delicious torment of his soft lips now searing a path down the center of her body. He wasn't the only one who had anticipated this moment, the time when they'd come together as one. Dreams of them making love had invaded her sleep more times than she could count.

He cupped one of her breasts in his large hand and his mouth covered her harden nipple. Licking, sucking, stroking, the flame burning inside her. The lust-arousing sensation he elicited had her core throbbing, eagerness built within her body. As he paid homage to her other breast, Jada squirmed beneath him, her fingers gripping his hair, waves of ecstasy whipping through her body. Oh yeah, this is what she wanted, what she craved.

Her body quivered everywhere he touched. His sinewy muscles contracted with every move he made. When Jada first met Zack, she never thought their initial attraction for each other would lead to the type of love that filled her heart. She was so glad he hadn't taken no for an answer when he first asked her out.

Zack slowly lifted his head and placed a lingering kiss against her lips before pulling away. The urge to pull him back, to feel his body above hers was strong, but she waited. Patience had never been one of her strengths, especially when her body yearned for him.

Her gaze followed as Zack leaned over to grab a condom

from the bedside table. She zoned in on his long, thick erection and her body pulsed with expectancy, eager to have him inside her.

Zack quickly sheathed himself and returned to her, picking up where he'd left off. Hovering above her, his hands on either side of her head, he reclaimed her lips, gently nudging her thighs apart.

"I want you so bad," he mumbled against her mouth, his voice raspy with unrestricted passion. His tongue traced the fullness of her lips, and he kissed her tenderly as the engorged head of his shaft teased her opening. A fiery sensation flowed through Jada like warm honey, and she bucked against him, needing him inside her.

She snatched her mouth from his. "Zack!" Her hands gripped his butt unable to handle anymore of his teasing. "I need you," she whimpered, not caring that her words sounded like she was begging.

"Ah, sweetie, I need you too." He eased into her, burying himself to the hilt, stretching her interior walls. Jada gasped, tightening her grasp on his butt. Heart beating wildly as he moved inside her, she gazed into his passion-filled eyes. His words from earlier filled her heart. *I love you.* And she loved him too, more than she ever thought possible.

Zack rocked his hips, slow and steady at first, but quickly picked up speed as he glided in and out of her slick heat. Her hips arched off the bed, catching his rhythm and matching his moves stroke for stroke. The erotic feel of him pulsing inside of her was like nothing she had ever experienced, and she didn't want him to stop, ever.

Jada grabbed hold of his sweat covered biceps, her nails digging into his skin, the turbulence from his thrusts growing more intense. In sync, they maintained the tempo that bound their bodies together. Their moans mingled, bounced off the walls, and filled the room with a lyrical tune that had her body humming with pleasure.

"Oh yes." Her breaths came in short spurts as she teetered

on the edge of an orgasm. "Za…" His name caught in her throat. Her pulse pounded in her ear, and the cyclone building up speed whirling on the inside slammed against her sweet spot and sent her tumbling over the edge of control. "Zack!" she cried, her body shuddered beneath him as she clung to his thick arms, falling, spiraling, and landing into contented bliss.

Not giving her time to recover, Zack's thrusts came harder, faster going deeper and his moves jerkier. With one last powerful thrust and a low, rumbling growl, his body convulsed uncontrollably and rocked the king sized bed like a six-point-five magnitude earthquake. Breathing hard, he collapsed on top of her. Seconds past before he rolled to his side taking her with him.

They both lay panting. Jada's chest heaved, and her body tingled from the most tantalizing lovemaking she'd ever experienced.

"Like I said earlier, you're remarkable," Zack mumbled, his head resting in the crook of her neck, his breath warm against her skin. They laid that way for the longest, and Jada knew without a doubt that there was no other place she would rather be than in his arms.

***

Zack left the bathroom and returned to the bed, pulling Jada close. He kissed the crown of her head wondering if she had caught his words earlier. He loved her. *I'm in love with this wonderful woman*. She touched something deep inside of him, and he couldn't think of anyone else he'd rather be with.

He caressed her arm, loving the feel of her soft skin. "What are you thinking about?"

"I still can't believe what you did for me."

"Well, baby, there's more where that came from." He nuzzled her neck and would have kept going if she hadn't pushed against his shoulder.

"Not that!" She giggled. "The clothes and accessories in

the other room. I can't believe I'm about to say this, but it's too much, Zack. I might love clothes, but even I have to admit that buying all of that stuff was way beyond—"

"Sweetheart, I wanted to do that for you. Thanks to me and my great date ideas, I'm sure you had to replace several items. The least I could do was help. Besides, the look on your face when you walked into the room was worth the effort."

"Still, it's too much." Jada's soft hands caressed his chest, sending desire to a particular part of his body that was longing to be back inside of her. He placed his hand over hers to stop the delightful torture.

"So let me ask you. Why didn't you want to go out with me when I first tried to get with you?"

Jada hesitated. "You unnerve me."

"What?" Zack chuckled. "How so?" He pushed strands of her hair away from her face.

Meeting his gaze, she said, "I like being in control of situations as well as my emotions. I felt out of control, from the moment I met you it was as if you were sucking away all of my power."

Zack laughed. "Are you serious?"

"Yes, I'm serious." She shoved him. "You make me feel things I have never felt for a man before and that's scary." Zack listened, surprised by her admission. "But I'm glad I finally said yes. I would've missed out on getting to know a wonderful man. You took good care of me during our dates. I'm fairly independent, but it's nice to have a man who comes to my rescue when I need him."

"I like taking care of you."

Zack twirled a lock of her hair around his finger. Jada, a woman who hated getting dirty and hated the outdoors, sacrificed her comfort for him. No woman had ever done anything for him that was so selfless.

"I have always wanted to share my love for sports and my love for the great outdoors with the women I've dated."

Jada looked up at him, and he placed a kiss on her lips. "You were the first woman who ever showed an interest in anything that interested me. Granted you weren't *really* interested."

"Well I…" He placed a finger on her lips to silence her.

"Though you weren't interested, you went anyway. Even almost got yourself killed a couple of times. Sweetheart, you don't know how much that means to me. Well, not the almost killing yourself part, but the selfless part. The part that didn't care that your expensive tennis shoes were ruined, or that you had to get a manicure twice one week because I had you digging around in dirt, picking vegetables. You probably have no idea how special that makes you, that you put me and my desires first."

"Zack … I need to tell you th—"

"You don't have to say anything. I'm cool with you not wanting to go fishing or hiking again, but I love that you did those things for me." He pulled her on top of him, her soft curves molding to the contours of his body. "But how is it that a sheet metal worker doesn't love the outdoors and has a problem getting dirty?"

"Well, I'm not your typical construction worker."

"Nooo!" he said in mock surprise. "I hadn't noticed."

"Shut up." She grinned and punched him in the shoulder. Turning serious, she ran her fingers through his hair. "I got into construction for a couple of reasons. One, I didn't want to go to college, and my parents made it clear that I had to do something because I couldn't live off of them for the rest of my life. And two, my brothers and my cousins were working in the family business. I figured I should too. Peyton was looking to get another sheet metal apprentice, and since I was always good in math, she suggested that I take the test."

"And then you became a sheet metal worker."

She nodded. "One thing led to another, and before I knew it, I had finished my five-year apprenticeship and I was a certified sheet metal worker."

"I'm impressed."

"Don't be. It's a dirty job, but someone has to do it." She cupped his face between her hands and kissed his lips. "There's something I want to ask you."

When she didn't continue, he leaned back a little, his head brushing against his pillow. "What? What do you want to ask me?"

"I just…"

He placed his finger under her chin, forcing her to look at him. "You just what?"

She stared at him, a hopeful glint in her eye. "Did you mean what you said earlier, about loving me?"

Ah, so she did catch that. "Yeah, I did. But if you don't feel the sa—"

"I do." Her soft hand caressed his cheek. "I love you too."

She giggled when he flipped her onto her back, nuzzling her neck. "Hmm, maybe we should show one another how much we love each other then."

CHAPTER ELEVEN

The next morning, Zack woke up to the ringing of his cell phone. He didn't care what time it was, all he knew is that it was too damn early for the phone to be ringing.

He started to reach for it on the bedside table, but Jada was lying on his chest, her legs intertwined with his. When the intrusive ringing stopped, he glanced at the clock. *Seven-thirty*. The only people who called him that early in the morning were Donny or Zack's mother, and he was sure that neither of them wanted anything.

Jada moaned and snuggled closer, her arm draped over him. He kissed the top of her head, playing with the ends of her hair. He could easily get used to having her in his arms and his bed every day.

The night before had been one of the most amazing nights of his life. Never had he connected with a woman, on so many levels, the way he had with Jada. This was what he wanted. She was who he wanted in his life.

He cursed under his breath when his cell phone started ringing again. This time he reached over and grabbed it.

"Yeah," he answered in a whisper.

"I take it this is a bad time," his oldest brother, Shane,

said.

"Yeah, it is."

"When's a good time to call back?"

Zack wanted to say never, knowing his brother only called that early in the morning if he wanted money or tickets to a game. "In a couple of hours."

"All right." He hung up without saying bye.

Zack put the phone back on the side table. He and Shane had a love-hate relationship that Zack had thought at one point would never survive. Zack loved him, but hated his attitude, especially when he acted as if everybody owed him something.

Readjusting the pillow behind him, Zack glanced down. Jada's almond shaped eyes stared up at him.

A smile immediately covered his lips. "Hey sweetheart, I'm sorry I woke you." He kissed her.

"Good morning." Jada stretched and yawned, but quickly covered her mouth. "Oh, sorry." She rolled to the other side of the bed.

"Hold up." Zack reached over and grabbed her by the waist, pulling her back to him. "Not so fast"

"I'm going to brush my teeth so that I don't knock you out."

He laughed and kissed her again. "I can handle a little morning breath if you can." Sighing with contentment, she settled against him, her head back on his chest.

"Did you sleep okay?" He moved his hand up and down her bare arm.

"Yeah. You wore me out."

Zack grinned, replaying some of the scenes from the night before in his mind. If he had any doubt that he and Jada were compatible in every area, that doubt was wiped away the day before. They hashed out their miscommunication and shared their bodies with each other proving again, how well they fit.

"So what do you think about us staying in bed for the rest

of the day?"

She glanced up at him. "I would love to, but I have a ton of things to do, including laundry. So I'm going to need to get home soon."

"Speaking of home. Tell me about your living arrangement."

"My living arrangement?" she asked confused.

"Yeah, why are you living with Christina?" He readjusted them, so they were both laying on their sides facing each other, his hand resting on her hip.

Jada thought about his question, debating on how to answer. Only Christina knew what type of debt she had accumulated and Jada planned to keep that secret to herself. But she didn't want to lie to Zack anymore.

"For a while I was renting a condo." She rubbed her hand slowly against his chest, enjoying the way his muscles contracted under her touch. "When I decided that I wanted to purchase one in the Hyde Park area, I mentioned it to CJ. Seeing that it was taking me a while to save up the cash, she offered to let me move in with her until I had enough money to purchase one." Jada stopped moving her hand and met his gaze. "Let's just say that I'm still saving."

"How much more do you need?"

Jada narrowed her eyes at him. "Why?"

"Because I can help you with the rest." His hand caressed her cheek, and she struggled to keep her eyes open due to how good he was making her feel. Each time he touched her, desire shot through her body wanting him to touch her in other places.

"I couldn't take that type of money from you." *Whoa! Did that just come out of my mouth?*

Jada shook her head slightly and lowered her gaze. She had changed. He might've been good husband material, but she wouldn't treat this relationship as she did others. No, Zack meant way more to her than using him for his money.

Zack's fingers sifted through her hair. "I'll admit that I've been burned a few times. People used me for my money. But you and I, this feels different. You're very important to me, Jada. So know that I wouldn't offer you something that I couldn't deliver on."

Jada's gaze had zoned in on his lips before her eyes met his intense ones. "I'm sure you could deliver on whatever you offer me, but money is not what I want from you."

"Hmm, is that right?" He cupped one of her breasts, squeezing gently as he ran his thumb across her perky nipple. Jolts of pleasure shot through her body to the tips of her toes. "Then what do you want from me?" He lowered his head to her breast and took her nipple into his mouth. Teasing. Licking. Sucking.

Everything within Jada turned to mush, and she knew she couldn't handle much more of his sweet torture. Bracing her hands on the side of his face, she tugged on him, forcing him to meet her eyes. She pulled him closer until their mouths were only an inch apart.

"All I want is you."

"That's good, because I'm all you'll ever need." He kissed her lips, and Jada could feel his love pouring through his touch as he stared into her eyes. "Move in with me," he said out of nowhere.

"What?"

"I want you to move in with me. I have plenty of space." He pushed her thick hair away from her face. "You already have a dressing room here. You might as well move in."

Jada leaned back and stared up at him, her mouth slightly open. When he didn't say more, she said, "Are you serious?"

"Yeah, I am."

"We don't even know each other that well."

"I know everything I need to know about you." He moved on top of her, careful not to put his full weight on her, placing a kiss on her forehead. "I'm looking for long term here, Jada, and I want that with you. Besides, you love me, and I love you. Why not take what we have to the next level.

Move in with me." He captured her lips and kissed her passionately, taking her breath away.

Jada didn't think she'd ever get tired of the way he worshiped her mouth. Taking what he wanted, yet giving her everything she needed.

"And while you're thinking about it, why don't I show you what you can expect every morning."

"Hmm," she moaned when he nudged her thighs apart and settled between her legs, "yes, why don't you."

***

Jada walked into Christina's house feeling like a new woman. Decked out in a Valentino pants suit with boots to match, she still had a hard time believing that Zack had surprised her with a new wardrobe. As a person used to receiving gifts from men, she could easily admit that yesterday's gift from him was the best by far. Yet, the thought of moving in with him had her reeling. She couldn't wait to tell Christina.

She followed the bumping noises coming from the kitchen.

"Christina I'm home! You are not going to believe this, but Zack asked me to move in with him!" She rounded the corner and stopped in her tracks.

Oh crap!

"Mom! What are you doing here? Where's CJ?"

"Actually I came to check on you." Kirsten Jenkins slammed the refrigerator door and turned to face Jada. "When I called yesterday, CJ told me you weren't feeling well. Imagine my surprise when I get here this morning and not only are you not here, but you didn't come home last night. *And* now I hear that you're planning to move in with some guy. Some guy your father and I haven't met, I might add."

"I didn't say I was moving in with him. I said he *asked* me to move in with him." She wanted to kick herself for shouting out her news before actually seeing Christina. Their family didn't stop by a lot but often enough that she should've known that she and CJ might not be alone.

"Did he also ask you to marry him? Because I know you are not thinking about moving in with someone without being married to him. And I know this because that's how your father and I raised you."

"But Toni—"

"Toni is not my child." Her mother's eyes were ablaze, and her hands propped on her hip. Jada knew Kirsten Jenkins was just getting warmed up. "We're talking about you! How could you consider moving in with someone before you're married?"

"Mom."

"Don't you mom me." She seemed to get madder by the minute. "Jada I'll admit we probably spoiled you giving you everything you wanted, but I know I can't stand by and let you do something like this. You're a beautiful, intelligent woman who deserves so much more. You don't have to settle for less than what I know you deserve."

They stood in silence for a minute. Jada tried to think of something that would diffuse the tension in the room. She and her mother were more similar than not with their style of dress, their personality, and their love for family. Their only difference was how they viewed life. Jada was a fly-by-the-seat of her pants person. Her mother planned everything. By the time Kirsten attended middle school, she had known what college she would attend, when she'd get married, how many children she would have, and when she would have them. Jada's original life plan was to find a wealthy man and live happily-ever-after shopping.

Jada lowered her eyes and picked some invisible lint from the sleeve of her jacket. She wasn't settling for less than she deserved and hoped when her mother met Zack, she'd see that. As a matter of fact, Zack was more than she could have ever hoped for.

"Aunt Kay." Jada heard Christina's voice heading in their

direction. "I checked but I … uh," she stuttered when she saw Jada, "Uh, I'm just going to…" She quickly turned to leave, but Kirsten's firm voice halted her.

"No. You're not going anywhere young lady. You're going to stay right there and tell me why you lied to me."

"Auntie—"

"She didn't lie," Jada said quickly. She couldn't let her cousin get into trouble covering for her. "I *was* sick yesterday. Uh … when we were out last night, we ran into Zack and Craig. When Zack found out I wasn't feeling well, he took me to his place since it was clos—"

"Save it, JJ." Kirsten snatched a cardboard box sitting on the counter near the back door and brought it to the center island. "I wasted my time making this soup thinking you were sick and then missed an important meeting in order to bring it to you." She placed a thick towel in the box before setting the large pot from the stove inside.

For the first time since walking into the kitchen, Jada noticed the familiar aroma.

"Mom," Jada worked up the nerve to approach her mother, "I appreciate you making my favorite soup. Don't take it back. I'll eat it."

Growing up, Jada couldn't ask for a better mother. For Kirsten, her family came first and to this day, she still hadn't stopped catering to their needs. Whether it was Jada's father not being able to find something around the house or one of her brothers caught up in some mess, the problem didn't matter. Kirsten always came to the rescue.

"I'm sorry I wasn't here when you arrived." Jada looped her arm through her mother's and rested her head against her shoulder. Something she often did as a kid knowing it would soften her mother's wrath.

Kirsten sighed softly and kissed the top of her daughter's head before stepping out of Jada's grasp.

"I love you and dad so much. Personally I think you guys did a great job raising me." Her mother rolled her eyes and took the pot back out of the box. Jada paced around the roomy kitchen trying to think of something to appease her mother.

Glancing toward the kitchen entrance, she saw that her cousin had disappeared from the room. Jada couldn't much blame her.

"Jada, before you start trying to pull your little spiel together, don't bother. You're an adult capable of making your own decisions. But I wouldn't be your mother if I didn't tell you how I feel about this new development." She poured the soup into a couple of smaller containers. "I don't like the idea of you shacking up with some man."

"His name is Zack."

She stopped and glared at Jada. "I don't care what his name is. He's still a man that I don't know and haven't met."

Jada couldn't wait for her parents to meet Zack. Whether she moved in with him or not, Jada knew that she and Zack would be together and maybe even get married someday.

"Mom, I respect your opinion. I have never wanted to disappoint either of you, but this is a decision I have to make for myself. You don't have to agree with what I decide, but I hope you'll be able to respect my decision." *And I hope that I don't make the same mistakes that I made with Dion.*

CHAPTER TWELVE

Zack gazed out the car window, watching as they passed vehicles and buildings along the highway in a blur. He was on his way to pick up Jada from her house, well Christina's house. Jada still hadn't given him an answer about moving in with him, but he wouldn't push. As long as they continued to spend as much time as possible together.

When Zack tried to pull his cell phone from his pocket, he winced and cursed under his breath. His bruised ribs from practice a couple of days earlier were still giving him problems. For the most part, he was fine, but every so often, he felt a twinge that reminded him that he wasn't a hundred percent. Had Jada not been looking forward to their evening out, he would have suggested doing something at home so that he could rest up.

A smile spread across his lips. Jada had shocked him when she invited him out to dinner, as well as to see a Broadway show downtown. Never had a woman offered to treat him to dinner and a show. Definitely a first.

The driver pulled in front of the small bungalow and parked.

"I got this Frank," he said to the driver, stopping him

before he climbed out of the driver's seat. "Be back in a minute."

Zack eased out of the vehicle, adjusted his bowtie, and fastened the single button of his black Armani suit. It had been awhile since he had dressed up. Something he didn't enjoy, but tonight Jada was calling the shots. Since she wanted him dressy, he would give her dressy.

He rang the doorbell and seconds later, the door opened. His breath caught in his throat as his gaze traveled the length of her body. He took in her long thick hair, curled at the ends, and hanging just past her shoulders. The sleek red dress that wrapped around her luscious curves and stopped a few inches above her knees screamed 'take me now'. Jada JJ Jenkins was one of the most beautiful women he'd ever met, but tonight the sexy vixen had the blood in his head flowing south at record speed.

Zack released a long, piercing whistle between his lips before he could stop himself. Words escaped him. Watching the way her gaze took in his apparel, appreciation glittering in her eyes was enough to make him want to take her right then, and there.

"Wow!" she finally said and stepped closer. Her hands did a slow glide up his chest, sending his libido into overdrive. Zack knew that if they didn't leave for the restaurant immediately they weren't going. Instead, he was going to lift her in his arms and carry her to the nearest bedroom.

"Jada," he said tightly, warning in his voice.

Ignoring his tone, she wrapped her arms around his neck. "Mr. Anderson, I must say, you clean up *very* nicely. I hope you're ready for a night you'll never forget."

Loving her boldness, he snaked his arms around her tiny waist, pulling her close, wanting her to relish the effect she was having on him. He rubbed his pelvis against her softness. "Any time with you is unforgettable."

He lowered his head and his mouth covered hers,

devouring the tenderness of her lips. A jolt of desire shot through him like a seventy-mile-per-hour tornado taking out everything in its wake. How could one kiss rock his world the way this one was rocking him? The feel of her lips against his felt like home.

His hands had a mind of their own as they slowly glided over her hips and landed on her firm butt. A moan pierced the air and Zack didn't know if the throaty sigh came from her or him and at the moment, he didn't care. All he knew was that the combustible yearning roaring through his body bordered on unbearable.

"Uh, you guys need to either bring that inside or take it outside. But whatever you do, close my door," Christina said from some place nearby. Zack wasn't sure since he wasn't ready to end the intense lip-lock. "You're letting the heat out!"

Both were slow to respond to Christina's reprimand. Jada eased her grip from around his neck, and he moved his hands up to her waist. "I'm not ready to let you go," Zack mumbled against her lips.

"And I'm not ready for you to let me go." She gave him one last kiss before stepping away, giving him a firsthand view of her backless dress and perfectly round ass.

Good Lord!

Jada grabbed her handbag and a Kate Spade jacket from a small table in the foyer. "Maybe we can pick this up in the car or after dinner. Or better yet, why don't we have a little dinner, go to the theater, and then finish this up at your place tonight."

He tugged on the handle of her bag, forcing her to him then lowered his head to her ear and whispered. "How is that better? Why don't we just skip dinner and the theater and just head straight to my place?"

She leaned back, placed her hand on her hip, and batted her long eyelashes. "Sorry, babe, but this dress," her hand slid from the side of her breast down past her hip, "is meant to be seen." Flashing a wicked smile that only made Zack more aroused, she looped her arm through his and pulled him out the door.

How in hell was he supposed to sit through dinner and a show with her in that dress and knowing she had big plans for him once they made it back to his place?

Frank stood on the passenger side with the back door of the vehicle opened.

"Thank you." Jada climbed into the town car. Zack didn't miss the way her short dress rode up her leg showing off her tempting thighs. If the tightness behind his pant zipper was any indication, it was going to be a long night.

Jada gave the driver the name of the restaurant and Zack settled in for the twenty-minute ride downtown.

"Getting a car and driver was a nice touch." She snuggled closer to him, and he groaned from the pain in his side, but wrapped his arm around her shoulder. He placed a kiss near her temple.

"I forgot about your ribs." Jada pulled away, but he tugged her back. "Are you sure you're up for having dinner and going to a show tonight? We can do this some other time."

He shook his head. "Sweetheart tonight is all about you. I'm used to the aches and pains."

"What about the plans I have for you later?" She played with the buttons on his shirt. Even in the semi-dark interior of the car, he could see the wicked gleam in her eyes. "Are you gonna be able to hang?"

"I have no doubt. Even busted up all over, my body would still respond to your sensuous touch." He lowered his head to her ear inhaling her intoxicating scent. He placed tiny kisses along her neck, deciding to mark his territory. Her moans only encouraged him to proceed. "I don't think I'll ever be able to get enough of you," he mumbled against her neck.

"Zack." She squirmed but didn't pull away. "You're

making it very hard to resist you."

He chuckled. "Good. My plan is working."

"Well, you need to save your plan for later. We're almost at the restaurant." She pressed her hands against his chest. "So behave."

Stealing another kiss, he leaned back in his seat thinking he couldn't wait to get her home. He grabbed hold of her hand, not able to stop himself from touching her in some way. When she turned slightly, the moonlight shone through the windows bestowing an angelic glow around her.

"God you're beautiful." He hadn't planned to say it yet again, but the words just tumbled out of his mouth.

"Thank you." She smiled and squeezed his hand. "Tell me you haven't seen Wicked yet."

He released her hand and put his arm around her neck. His fingers sifted through the length of her soft hair hanging down her back. Donny had once told him that a black woman's hair was off limits, but Jada didn't seem to mind him playing in hers.

"I haven't seen the show yet. Actually, I can't remember the last time I've gone to the theater." The moment the words left his mouth, the memory of him and Leslie leaving a Broadway show in New York popped into his head. That weekend was when she had asked to borrow some money for her brother Caleb, who was trying to start a limousine service business. Zack and Leslie had been arguing more and more, and red flags regarding their relationship were starting to pop up. He wasn't giving her brother a dime. From the moment, Zack had met him he knew he was a hustler trying to make a quick buck. And when the bank contacted him about the check Leslie was trying to cash, he knew he was done with her.

"Zack?" Jada squeezed his thigh. When he looked at her, he noticed the concern in her, brown eyes. "You okay?"

He ran the back of his fingers down her cheek. The tenderness in her eyes made him want to say the hell with dinner, but he couldn't do that to her. Not after the funky dates he'd taken her on over the past couple of months.

"As long as I'm with you, I'm perfectly fine." He nibbled on her lower lip, then her top one. He could spend the rest of his life kissing her and be perfectly content.

"Hmm, pouring on the charm are we."

He grinned and kissed her again. His hand rested on her thigh, loving the feel of her silky, soft skin beneath his touch. Trying not to think about all the wicked things he planned to do to her back at his place was going to be nearly impossible.

They neared the downtown restaurant and nightclub, Zydeco, Cincinnati's new hotspot. His driver fell in line behind other cars as the valets hustled from one vehicle to the next. Zack mentally prepared himself for the onslaught of people as small groups were gathered at the door. He assumed people were waiting to be seated in the restaurant considering the club didn't open until ten. He hated crowds almost as much as he hated wearing a stuffy suit and tie. But seeing Jada's excited face, he'd suck it up for her. Tonight was all about what she wanted.

"I made reservations," Jada pulled out a mirror and finger combed her hair before stuffing the mirror back into her handbag. "By the looks of that line, I hope we don't have to wait."

"Whose name did you put the reservation under?" he asked, glancing out the window. Already he was having second thoughts about this particular restaurant, knowing that it had been in the news recently for the crowds getting out of control. Several of his teammates had had their share of trouble hanging out at other nightclubs, and Zack wasn't trying to be added to that list.

"I put the reservation in your name."

"Good. We won't have to wait."

She narrowed her eyes at him, a half smile on her lips. "Oh, so what, you being a famous football player in this town carries that much weight?" Humor laced her words. "How do you know we won't have to wait?"

"Because I know the owner." He smiled and wiggled his eyebrows, eliciting a burst of laughter from her.

Frank opened the back door, and Zack stepped out, ignoring the burning of his ribs. He reached back for Jada's hand to help her out of the car and informed their driver that he would text him when they were ready to leave.

"Isn't that the football player who's in those car commercials all the time?" Someone to the side of them whispered.

"Zack Anderson! How ya doin', man?" A fan extended his hand and Zack shook it, nodded his head at the guy, and kept moving toward the hostess stand. The last thing he wanted was to bring attention to himself. He gripped Jada's hand when it seemed as if there were more people huddled together as he neared the hostess.

"Hey, Zack Anderson! Can I get a photo with you?"

After a moment, Zack half-heartedly agreed to a photo with the fan and his family, deciding that was the only one he'd agree to. All the attention reminded him of why he tried to stay out of the public's eye. The moment they finished taking the photo, he pulled Jada to his side and whispered in her ear. "Sorry about that."

"No problem." She rubbed his lower back, her other hand on his chest.

"Good evening," the petite hostess, with a short curly afro greeted. "Welcome to Zydeco. Do you have a reservation?"

Zack gave his name to the hostess and glanced around the trendy spot. To their right, people crowded around a large circular bar or sat at tables lacing the perimeter of the sectioned off space. On the opposite side of the restaurant sat a platform holding six semi-circular booths with high back velvet benches. It was clear the restaurant had good business. The tables and smaller booths in the center of the huge space were occupied.

"All right Mr. Anderson, if you'll step over here," she pointed to a spot to her right where another couple was waiting, "we'll show you to your table shortly."

"Well, if it isn't *the* Zachary Anderson, Cincinnati's king of the football field. What's up with you boy?"

Zack turned to the gruff voice that could only belong to one person. He grinned at his college friend, Randy Mills, owner of Zydeco restaurant and nightclub. Zack reluctantly released Jada's hand to shake Randy's and pulled him in for a one-arm hug, pounding him on his back.

"What's up, man?" Zack was glad to see his longtime friend. "You a greeter now? I thought you'd be in the back bossing people around or something."

They both laughed. "Nah, I saw your name on the list earlier and figured I'd come out and see you." He turned to Jada. "Zack, I see you still have good taste when it comes to women."

Zack put a possessive arm around her waist, pulling her closer to his side. "This is my lady, Jada Jenkins. Jada meet Randy Mills one of the smartest and loudest guys I know. He's also the owner of Zydeco."

"Nice to meet you." He shook Jada's hand, holding on to it a little too long as far as Zack was concerned.

"Nice to meet you too. You have a beautiful place here." Jada waved her hand at their surroundings.

"Thank you. I've been trying to get your man here to stop by. So I assume I have you to thank for his presence."

Jada wrapped her arm around Zack's waist. She smiled up at him. There was something special and sexy in her gaze that made him feel as if he could leap a building in a single bound. He couldn't ever remember a woman looking at him with such … he wasn't sure what he saw. Admiration? Respect? Love? He wasn't sure, but it stirred the lust that was already building within him.

She returned her attention to Randy. "I might have had a

little," she held her thumb and index finger close together, "bit of influence in getting him here." They all laughed.

Randy grabbed a couple of menus. "All right, let me see if my staff and I can show you a good time. Then maybe you'll come back again," he said to Zack. "I saved the best table in the house for you."

When they arrived at their table, in a quiet corner at the back of the restaurant, Zack pulled out Jada's chair before sitting in his own. He had to admit that the ambiance of the room, the dimmed lights, candlelit centerpieces on the tables, and the smooth sound of jazz flowing through the speakers was making a good impression. He wouldn't expect anything less from Randy though. His college friend always did do everything with style and finesse.

"Are you going to serve our meal too?" Zack asked when Randy handed them menus.

"Ha, ha, I see you have jokes." He shoved his hands into the pants pocket of his tan, tailored suit. "Your server will be here shortly, but I have to ask what I know everyone is dying to know, Zack. What's this I hear about you retiring at the end of the season?"

Zack shook his head. When he renewed his contract with Cincinnati for only one year, speculations about him leaving the game spread like a wild fire. Yes, he was thinking about retiring, but he hadn't made a definite decision yet.

Before Zack could respond, Randy said, "Don't do it, man. Cincinnati needs you. Besides, you're still somewhat young. Why give up the game now when you're in your prime?"

Glad that the dining tables were spread far apart enough for others not to hear their conversation, Zack explained. "Between us Randy, I haven't made any definite decisions. I won't lie and say I haven't been thinking about retirement. When I leave the game, I want to leave while I still have my faculties and the ability to walk off the field on my own." He rubbed his jaw and chin. "You know how it is, man. I've been at this ten years. As a running back, my body won't be able to continue to take the pounding that it gets every week out on that field." Zack stopped speaking and looked at Jada, who was studying him carefully. He rapped his larger hand around her smaller one that rested on the table. "Besides, I have to start thinking about my future. Getting married and starting a family."

CHAPTER THIRTEEN

Jada almost fell out of her chair and puddled to the floor at Zack's words. His crystal blue eyes didn't stray from hers, and she had no doubt he was serious about what he said. Sure, he had asked her to move in, but he hadn't said anything about the possibility of marriage.

Zack removed his hand from hers, and she immediately missed the warmth that his touch always radiated through her body.

"With all that said, I haven't made any definite decisions," he said to his friend.

Randy gripped Zack's shoulder. "I have mad respect for you, man. Whether you stay on with Cincinnati or leave, you've had one helluva career."

The server came over, and Randy said his goodbyes, promising to see them before they left. The server left the table after taking their drink orders.

Zack reached for Jada's hand again and leaned in close. "I hope I didn't embarrass you a few minutes ago. I shouldn't assume that we want the same thing."

For the first time in a long time, Jada didn't know what to say. How many times had she imagined a man including her in his plans that possibly led to marriage?

She squeezed his hand. "I think we do want the same thing."

Those dimples of his that always made her heart flutter appeared, and he moved even closer to her. "Is that right?"

She grinned and nodded. He lowered his head and captured her lips in a kiss that made her toes curl. She didn't think she'd ever get used to his sweetness and the touch of his mouth against hers.

Once the server took their order and left them with warm bread, Zack shared stories of him and Randy from when they were back in college. Jada couldn't believe some of the pranks they'd pulled and the type of trouble they got into their freshman year. Zack explained that when the school administrator threatened that Zack would lose his scholarship if he didn't straighten up, he and Randy didn't hang out as much. Zack put most of his energy into his schoolwork and left the rest out on the football field.

"So what did you major in?"

He laid the slice of bread that he had just bitten into on a small plate and wiped his mouth. "Finance for my undergrad and I have my MBA."

"Wow. That's wonderful." Jada thought of Zack as just a pro football player, forgetting he had a college education. "How or when did you get your MBA since you started playing pro football right after you graduated with your bachelors?"

"I did an accelerated MBA program, completing some of the courses online and attending classes during the off season. It was supposed to be accelerated, but it took me about two and a half years because of my football schedule."

"I'm impressed."

Jada pushed down the anxiety churning in her stomach. Over the years, she had had plenty of time to continue her education, but hadn't. Going to college wasn't one of her life goals, but now she wondered if she should rethink her goals.

Would Zack one day feel the same as Dion had – claiming that all she had to bring to the table were her good looks and a tight body? Granted the two men were very different people, but she couldn't help but wonder.

"Growing up in one of the roughest neighborhoods in Columbus, I had vowed that I was going to make something of myself. I knew I wanted to play professional football, but I also knew there were plenty of other guys that were just as talented. The competition was steep. So I had to get an education or take up a trade. I—"

He stopped speaking when the server brought their food to the table. Jada wasn't very hungry, but her mouth watered when the steaming hot plate was set before her. Crab stuffed shrimp and one of her weaknesses, mashed potatoes. Glancing at Zack's plate of bourbon glaze salmon, she was tempted to dig her fork into the fish for a taste.

"Is there anything else I can get either of you?" the server asked, looking from Jada to Zack.

"Everything looks amazing."

"This looks great."

Zack and Jada spoke at the same time, eliciting a laugh from the server.

"Well, enjoy your meals and let me know if you need anything else."

Jada dug into her mashed potatoes. She felt like such an underachiever compared to Zack. As the youngest in her family and the only girl, her parents supplied her with whatever she wanted. She hadn't really thought much about her future. It was not until she decided that she didn't want to go to college did things change in their household. Her parents gave her an ultimatum. Either go to college or find a job. She couldn't live under their roof without one or the other. Becoming a sheet metal worker wasn't in her plans. It was not until she found out how much money construction workers made did she decide to pursue a career in the trades.

They ate and talked, enjoying each other's company. This

was what Jada had been missing with their previous dates. She had longed to get dressed up and go out on the town with Zack. Not just to be seen with a handsome man, but needing to have what she referred to as a real date. Their conversation flowed easily, and it was refreshing to be with a man who didn't talk about himself the whole time.

"What made you pick this restaurant?" Zack cut into his salmon. "Have you been here before?"

Jada shook her head, having just bit into one of the shrimps. "No, I've wanted to come since it opened. So when I thought about us going out for a nice dinner," she shrugged, "this was the first place I thought about. What's your excuse for not coming here sooner, especially since you know the owner?"

"No special reason. Only that I'm not a big fan of large crowds or popular, hotspots. This place has been getting rave reviews and is listed as one of the top ten places to be on the weekend in Cincinnati." He plopped a piece of the fish into his mouth and moaned. "Damn, this is good." He wiped his mouth. "You've been eying my plate ever since the server sat the dish in front of me. Do you want some?" He held his fork, loaded with salmon, in front of her.

Jada couldn't resist. She opened her mouth and the moment the succulent fish touched her tongue, she closed her eyes and moaned. The women in her family were excellent cooks, but this had to be the best salmon she had ever tasted.

"Oh my goodness, you're right." She opened her eyes, still chewing, only to find Zack staring at her, his eyes glittered with desire. She swallowed hard as he moved his chair closer to hers.

"Sweetheart, you can not moan like that and not expect to have an effect on me. Come here," he said, his voice raspy.

No more words were spoken. With his hand at the back of her head, he gently pulled her to him and covered her mouth with his. Jada didn't ever think she'd get tired of kissing him. Each time his lips touched hers, everything in her yearned for more. His tongue tangled with hers, and she placed her hand on his chest, his hard muscles contracting beneath her touch. When he increased the pressure of their kiss, longing shot through her like a rocket launching into interplanetary space. She squeezed her thighs together to control the sweet, torturous throb between her legs. She wanted him like she'd never wanted any other man and tonight she couldn't wait to get him home.

Jada saw a flash and lifted her head. When she and Zack pulled apart, they both noticed a man standing about ten feet from their table, his cell phone in his hand. He snapped another picture.

"What the fu…" Zack bolted from his seat, knocking over his chair before Jada could stop him. He grabbed the man by the front of his shirt. "What the hell are you doing?" Zack snatched the cell phone out of the guy's hand and held it out of his reach.

"Hey, give me that back!" The man flailed his arms trying to reach his phone as Zack maintained a death grip on the guy's shirt, keeping him at arm's length.

"Zack, you're making a scene," Jada whispered, trying to get him to calm down. "Just give the phone back to him. It's not that serious."

"The hell it isn't," Zack growl. "You're going to delete every damn picture you took of us."

"It's a free country—"

"What's going on here?" Randy and someone from his security team came up to them, separating the two men. Security held the other patron, while Zack backed away until he was near their table.

"Zack, let's just go." Jada grabbed hold of his muscular arm while he pushed buttons on the man's cell phone, apparently deleting the photos himself. "Zack."

"Give me a minute," he said distractedly.

"What happened?" Randy asked Jada, who was still

holding onto Zack's muscular bicep, trying to ignore all of the stares. "What did the guy do?"

"He took photos of us kissing," Jada explained, glad to see that Zack was finished.

"Get him out of here," Randy said to security and followed behind them.

"Hey! What about my phone?" the man yelled as they escorted him out of the main dining room.

Jada normally enjoyed being the center of attention, but with the anger seeping through Zack's pores, all she wanted to do was get out of there. She had to admit, a stranger taking pictures of them was a little creepy. The last thing she needed or wanted was for someone to post pictures of them on the internet.

With the cell phone still in his hand, Zack tossed enough money on the table to cover the meals and a sizeable tip. They headed to the lobby, and she could tell by the grip he had on her hand and his clenched jaw that he was still mad.

"Zack, I'm sorry about all of that." Randy stopped him in the lobby, near the hostess stand, his hand on Zack's shoulder. He directed them to the far corner of the large space for privacy. "I feel bad about what happened. At least let me take care of your dinner."

"It's not your fault." He handed Randy the cell phone he'd taken from the other patron."

"Yeah, it is my fault. Anyone who steps foot in my restaurant should be able to have a nice dinner without being harassed by some misguided fan."

"Shit like this happens more times than I can count." Zack released Jada's hand and wrapped his arm around her, his hand resting on her hip. "I'm sure I could have handled it differently and maybe I would have if it were just me here." He glanced at Jada. Normally when he looked at her he was smiling. This time she couldn't read his expression. "I won't tolerate that type of disrespect when she's with me," he said to Randy. "By the way, the food and the service were excellent. All the best to you, man."

They said their goodbyes and Zack quickly texted the driver, but still hadn't said anything to Jada. Normally he seemed totally in control, but witnessing the way he sprang into action moments ago, surprised her. Maybe this incident was why he hadn't taken her to places like Zydeco for their dates. If this was what he went through whenever he was around people, she could see why he would shy away from public appearances.

With his hand at the small of her back, he guided her outside. Hundreds of people were lined up to enter the nightclub, which had a separate entrance. Jada was curious about the club, but not enough to talk Zack into checking it out with her.

"Zack Anderson!" someone yelled and Jada groaned.

"Nice game last week, Zack!"

She felt him stiffen next to her, not understanding why people calling out his name and expressing their love for him bothered him so much.

Suddenly a bright light flashed, temporarily blinding her and then another. She lifted her hands to block the lights and leaned into Zack, who had a tight hold on her, moving her quickly along the sidewalk.

"Zack, who's the new woman?"

"Are the retirement rumors true?"

Questions came from all directions. Jada felt as if they were on the red carpet for an award's show instead of hanging out at a restaurant.

An aggressive paparazzo stepped in front of them. Zack cursed under his breath. He winced in pain when he turned suddenly, taking her in a different direction, keeping her close by his side.

"Zack, your ex, Leslie Dunkin, just announced her engagement to Yuko Arizu." Someone shoved a microphone in his face, close to Jada's head, and she stumbled. "What do you think about–"

Zack grabbed the guy's wrist and shoved him. "Back the hell up!" he growled, holding Jada tighter, shielding her from the people blocking their path and the assault of camera flashes. That didn't stop the onslaught of questions. Jada kept her head burrowed into Zack's chest until he whispered. "There's Frank."

The driver parked a few feet away and jumped out of the car. Rounding the vehicle, he yanked the back door open. As soon as Jada breathed a sigh of relief, someone grabbed Zack's arm.

"Hey, how about an autograph?" Zack shook the guy off and released Jada.

"Get her in the car!"

Frank hustled her into the backseat and then jumped to Zack's defense just before Zack's fist made contact with a reporter's face, who had shoved the microphone at them earlier. "Let's go!" Frank yelled, pulling Zack back and shoving him into the vehicle.

"Dammit!" Zack pounded his fist against the interior of the car door. "That shit gets on my nerve!"

Adrenaline soared through Jada as she tried to catch her breath. Normally something like that scene would excite her but seeing the effect it had on Zack, made her wary. She couldn't imagine going through this every time she went out.

"Are you okay?" He cupped her chin with one hand, looking at her with concerned eyes. The tension radiating from him was freaking her out a little. Never had she seen him so riled up, yet the way he took charge was a serious turn on.

She nodded. "Yeah, yeah, I'm fine. Are you?" She heard the quiver in her own voice and was sure he hadn't missed it.

"I'm cool. I just don't like them getting in our face like that, especially in your face. I'm used to their aggression, but I never wanted you to have to experience it. Some of the media are not as considerate as the others and will stop at nothing, to get an answer or a reaction out of you."

"Like making you take a swing at them," Jada cracked. She watched him almost punch someone, which seemed so out of character for him.

"I'm sorry you had to witness that, but I won't apologize for wanting to knock the crap out of him." Snuggling up to Zack, she looped her arm through his and kissed him on the cheek. "He was too damn close to you with his microphone. I couldn't tell if he'd bumped you with it or not."

"He didn't and I'm fine. Thank you for taking care of me back there."

He placed a kiss on her forehead and slipped his arm out of her grasp, wrapping it around her shoulders. "I will always take care of you."

Frank cleared his throat. He had been driving, but Jada realized that they hadn't told him where to go.

"I'm sorry, Frank. We're going to call it a night. Drop us off at my place." Jada's shoulders drooped. She couldn't believe they were skipping the theater. When her gaze met Zack's, his eyes searched hers as if making sure she was okay with his decision.

Jada didn't say anything. She knew he'd had enough for one night and as long as they were together, it really didn't matter where they went next.

Zack lowered his head to her ear. "Are you okay with this?"

She nodded slowly.

"I'll reimburse you for the tickets and I promise I'll make this up to you." He placed a soft kiss against her lips. "And I really am sorry about all of that back there. I try never to lose my temper, but..." His voice trailed off as if he couldn't come up with a good reason for losing his temper.

"How do you think they knew we were there?" Jada straightened in her seat so that she could look at him better.

Zack moved his arm from around her shoulder and released an exhausted breath, running his hand over his short, spiked hair. "I'm not sure, but I wouldn't be surprised if Randy called them."

"What? Why?" Randy seemed like a nice guy. Jada couldn't see him doing anything so underhanded.

"Randy is trying to put his restaurant and night club on the map. If he can get some free publicity, I'm sure he'll do whatever it takes. What better way to draw more people out than to show them the professional athletes, actors, and models who patronize his establishment? Lines of people wrapped around the block waiting to get into the nightclub doesn't hurt either." Zack shrugged. "The commotion tonight will draw the grocery store tabloids, and people love drama. People will be clamoring to check out his spot. More money in his pocket."

"But you guys are friends. He'd do something like that to you?"

"*If* he did make a call, I know it's not personal. It's business … for him."

Jada mulled over their conversation and decided that she couldn't see putting one of her friends through some mess like that.

The magic of Alex Bugnon's talented fingers skimming over piano keys flowed through the speakers and Jada rested her head against Zack's shoulder and shut her eyes. Tonight felt like a real first date with him, despite the drama.

***

The next morning, Zack kissed Jada on the top of her head, and peeled himself out of her grasp. He climbed out of bed and stumbled into the master bathroom. He loved when she stayed the night, but leaving her in his bed sleeping was getting harder and harder. He wanted nothing more than to stay snuggled beside her, but duty called. The Cougars were scheduled to meet earlier than usual to lift weights.

Zack grabbed his toothbrush and the remote control to the television mounted in the corner near the second sink. His mother thought it a little excessive to have a television in the bathroom. He wasn't a big TV watcher, but he liked to watch one of the national sports stations to catch up on the latest in sports, while he got ready.

"Damn," Zack said when he saw the photo plastered across the television screen of him and Jada leaving the restaurant the night before. Brushing his teeth, he turned up the volume.

"Now here's someone we don't see in the news often. Last night Cincinnati Cougars' running back, Zack Anderson, was spotted leaving the popular restaurant and nightclub, Zydeco," the first announcer said.

"Terry, I think the last time we saw him in the news was over six months ago when his fiancée at the time, accused him of domestic violence. Granted it turned out to be untrue, but last night he was with an unidentified woman. It appears Anderson got a little hot under the collar with a paparazzo. Do we have a clip?"

Zack groaned when he watched himself on television lunging at a reporter. *Damn that was close.* Frank had grabbed his arm mid-swing and shoved Zack into the car. Whenever he needed a driver, he always requested Frank. As a former Marine, he was good at detecting problems before they happened. The last thing Zack wanted was his name attached to some nonsense, especially before he retired from the league.

Zack hoped none of his teammates saw the clip, but he knew that was wishful thinking.

An hour later, he strolled into the locker room. It seemed everyone had arrived before him, which was unusual.

"Well, well, well, if it isn't Mr. Photogenic," one of the defensive linemen said as Zack walked passed him to get to his locker. "All I want to know is who was the cutie pie you were with last night?"

"Rumor has it you're pretty serious about this woman."

"I heard she's a construction worker," someone across the room added.

"No way she works construction," another teammate

said.

Everyone added their two cents, but Zack kept walking, shaking off those who shoved him playfully. He dropped his duffle bag on the floor next to his locker and slipped out of his jacket. With all of the talk about Jada, his mind immediately backtracked to the previous night.

His lips tilted into a smile. She had stripped for him, and all thoughts of Zydeco, pushy fans, and aggressive paparazzi slid from his mind. Her love for sexy underwear showed in the numerous styles and colors she wore and the night before was no different. The look of the red satin and lace bra with the matching string-bikini would be forever embedded in his mind.

"You know what they say man," Becker, one of the team's offensive lineman interrupted his thoughts and pounded him on the shoulder, "once you go black, you never go back." Everyone burst out laughing. Zack shook his head and chuckled.

He turned his back to his teammates, who were still laughing and cracking jokes. Had it been anyone else, or a different group of men, he might have had a problem with the comment. Except these guys were the best. Closer than brothers, it wasn't uncommon for them to joke good-naturedly.

"I see my man still knows how to pick them."

"Does she have a sister," someone else asked.

This is going to be a long morning.

CHAPTER FOURTEEN

Days later, Zack stood at the wall-to-wall windows of his sunroom, looking out over his massive yard finding peace in the stillness of the night. Snow flurries blew around, but no accumulation was expected despite it being the first week of December. Cincinnati hadn't seen but a light dusting of snow the week prior, but Zack knew the flurries would soon turn to outright snow soon enough.

"You do realize this birthday party is for you don't you?" Carol Anderson, Zack's mother, asked from behind him.

He turned from the window to find her standing in the middle of the room holding a glass of wine. In her early sixties, his mother was still as young and vibrant as he remembered her to be during his childhood. Zack always appreciated her love for life despite all that she had experienced over the years. Somewhat eccentric in everything she did, she pushed the envelope, especially with her style of dress, even tonight. Her long reddish hair was the perfect accessory to her red rim glasses and red pinstripe suit with matching shoes.

"Why are you hanging out here by yourself? Is something wrong?"

"Everything is fine, Mom. I just came out for a little breather. It looks like you and Jada invited everyone and their mother."

"Is that what this is about? You're upset because we threw you a birthday party?" Her hand landed on her hip, and she shifted her weight to one leg. "Do you know how many people didn't live to see their thirty-third birthday? Every year is a gift from God."

"I know, Mom, and it's not that I don't appreciate the party. I love you and Jada for doing this for me."

"Life is too short. You have to celebrate every moment."

"Is that why you're marrying Haverty?"

"I thought you said you were okay with that."

Zack shoved his hands into his front pants pockets. "I never said I was okay with my mother committing immigration fraud. I get that you're trying to help your friend stay in the country, but marriage seems a little extreme. I want you to remarry, but I'd hoped you'd marry someone you loved, and someone who loves you."

"I don't think love is in the cards for me." She sipped her wine. "Although, I am glad you found love. The more time I spend with Jada, the more time I want to spend with her. She's such a sweetheart. She reminds me a little of myself."

Zack smiled. He recognized the similarities early on. Their love for family being the first thing he noticed. Over the past few months, he also noticed they both enjoyed shopping, eating out, and throwing parties.

"Haverty is very special to me. If he has to leave the country then I'd have to visit him all the time, and I don't want to do that. I'm hoping for some grandkids in the near future, so I need to stay close to Cincinnati, or wherever you and Jada will be." She winked.

"Mom, your *fiancé* looks like he's *really* having a good time with that champagne fountain." Shane smirked, his long blond hair falling in his face, over his left eye. Zack's oldest brother made it clear earlier when they received the news that he hated the idea of their mother remarrying.

Carol shook her head. "Gee, thanks, son." She swatted Shane's arm on her way out of the room.

"Happy birthday, little brother. You're doing it big this year." He nodded toward the glass wall, where they both could see into the kitchen and through to the family room. "There's a lot of folks here."

"Yeah, I know. I have Mom and Jada to thank for this," he said dryly. "What's up with you? How's the new job?"

"It's a job." He took a swig of his beer. "It's only been a month and already my boss is starting to act like an ass. I need to just go ahead and get my own thing going."

His brother had been in and out of work for the past three years. Zack was pretty sure his inability to hold onto a job had more to do with his brother's negative attitude more so than anything.

"Well, it's only been a month. Give it a chance."

"I guess. So um …" Shane looked down at his shoes before returning his attention to Zack, "I was wondering if I can use one of your spare rooms for a few weeks."

"What's wrong with your place? Why do you need to stay here?"

"Does it matter? You have more than enough space. I asked you for a place to stay, shouldn't your response be, sure, no problem?"

Zack folded his arms across his chest and studied his brother. Twice in the last eight months, Shane had moved into one of Zack's spare rooms, staying for a couple of months each time. Zack was okay helping his brother out occasionally, but lately Shane had been asking to borrow money, begging for football tickets, and borrowing his vehicles. Yet, he gave nothing in return. He never paid the money back, never offered to replace the gas he used, and walked in tonight with only a *happy birthday*. Now that Zack had asked Jada to move in, if she agreed, his brother would have to find someone else to mooch off of.

"Let me think about it."

His brother stiffened as if Zack had hit him. "Think about it? What the hell? Why you gotta think about it?"

Zack's attention immediately shifted to Jada, who walked into the kitchen and headed in his direction. His gaze traveled the length of her body. He still couldn't get over how *hot* she looked. Her dark gray, one shoulder dress that wrapped around her luscious curves did wicked things to his libido. Yet, it was her shoes that caused his mouth to drop open earlier. The matching stilettos with the rhinestone straps around her ankles were the sexiest shoes he'd ever seen on a woman.

"Shane, I'll think about it and get back to you."

"Zack—"

"Hey sweetheart," Zack said when Jada walked into the room. He ignored Shane's low growl as his brother stormed out without acknowledging Jada.

"I don't think he likes me." She stepped into Zack's waiting arms. "Every time he looks at me, I feel like running for cover."

"Forget him." Zack placed a lingering kiss on her cheek. "All that matters is that I love you."

She batted those long eyelashes and flashed that smile that always made him feel like the luckiest man alive.

"You're right, but I want your family to like me."

"My family does like you." He caressed her cheek, sensing that their acceptance of her was important. "My mother is already envisioning you as the mother of her future grandchildren. My sister considers you her sister from another mother, and my youngest brother wants to know if he can clone you."

She rewarded Zack with a smile. "That's sweet. I think they're pretty amazing too, but Shane—"

"It doesn't matter what he says or thinks. My heart belongs to you."

"Aw, Zack. You always know the right thing to say."

When her soft lips touched his, it was as if everything else disappeared. The phrase – she completes me – floated to the forefront of his mind. This amazing woman brought a level of peace in his life that he never knew he was missing.

Jada's small hands framed his face, bringing him back to the present when she ended their kiss. "Though I would love to keep kissing you, it's time to cut your cake."

"Instead of cake, I'd rather have you." Between the sexy outfit and her tantalizing scent, he was about ready to kick everybody out of his house, carry her upstairs, and have his way with her.

Zack planted soft kisses along her jaw and worked his way down her long, graceful neck. "You already have me," she said on a moan. He made it to her shoulder, but she stopped him. "If you can make it through another hour or two, I'll let you see my new underwear." She wiggled her eyebrows and eased out of his grasp.

He couldn't help but laugh. "What color are they?" He followed behind her like a puppy being promised a treat. "Are they see through, lace, what? You gotta give me something here."

"Oh, I have something for you alright, but not now. Later."

She pulled him into the huge dining room where many of his guests had piled into, while the rest spilled over into the attached formal living room.

"Well, it's about time," one of his teammates said.

Before he could respond with a smart remark, everyone started singing happy birthday. Zack appreciated Jada's and his mother's efforts, but he didn't like being the center of attention.

"Make a wish, baby." Jada nudged him closer to the table.

He snaked his arm around her narrow waist. "My wish has already come true." He kissed her as the women in the room released collective sighs, and the men groaned.

"He's a goner," someone behind him called out.

Zack blew out the candles to a round of applause. Still holding Jada close, he thanked everyone for coming and for celebrating with him. Maybe he didn't enjoy being the center of attention, but he did enjoy having his family and friends near.

Zack roamed around greeting people he hadn't yet spoken to and tried not to think about the birthday gifts that Jada had been promising him all evening. Since his team had a bye week, giving him four consecutive days off, he wanted to spend every one of them with Jada. He had tried talking her into going away for the weekend, but she and his mother had already planned his party.

He walked down to the lower level of his home where he had a theater, game room, and a lounge. Combined it was the man cave he'd always wanted. Surprised that there weren't as many people down there, he waltzed toward the door leading into the theater.

"Zack, look who just showed up."

Zack turned to the sound of Donny's voice and a grin spread across Zack's face.

"What's up, old dude?" Luke Hayden one of Zack's best friends from college shook his hand and pulled him in for a one-arm hug. "How's it feel to be a year older?"

Zack laughed. "I'm just glad to see another year, man. I wasn't expecting you in town for another couple of weeks. What's up with that?"

"I have an interview with a downtown law firm later this week."

"I can't believe you're thinking about leaving New York." Donny grabbed a hors d' oeuvre from a passing waiter and plopped it into his mouth. "How you gon' leave the big city of dreams?"

Luke chuckled and shrugged. "It's time."

Luke, an attorney, moved to New York right after college. Recently he had told Zack that with all of the loss that he had experienced in his life over the past few years, he was ready for a change and ready to leave New York. Leaving his fast-paced life for something quieter was all Luke talked about lately.

"I'm glad I was able to come to town a little early. Otherwise, I would've missed this big shindig you're having." He waved his hand around at the eloquent decorations. "Looks like you're finally spending some of that money you have stored away."

"Actually, my mother and Jada are spending it." They all laughed, and Zack was a little surprised that Donny hadn't made a crack about Jada since he thought she was high maintenance.

"So when am I going to meet this woman of yours? As much as you talk about her, I feel like I already know her."

Zack glanced around wondering where Jada had disappeared. "She's around here somewhere. Hey Craig, have you seen Jada?"

Craig walked toward them shaking his head. "Not for a while. What's up, Luke? I haven't seen you in over a year." They shook hands.

"I had to come and celebrate with this old guy." He nudged Zack. "But I hear congratulations are in order. Heard you got married."

Craig nodded. "Yep, Toni and I were married almost four months ago. She's the best thing that's ever happened to me."

"Sounds like you and Zack have both lucked out. I've known this guy," he pointed to Zack, "for years and have heard more about Jada than any other woman he's ever dated. I need to meet the person who has turned him into a big marshmallow."

"A marshmallow?" Zack punched him in the arm. "Really? Of all the things you could call me, that's all you could come up with?"

"Hey, I call it like I see it. She must be a helluva woman

145

to have you going on and on about her over the last few months."

"I'm surprised you didn't see her when you first came in," Craig said. "She and Toni were standing near the front door a few minutes ago."

"I saw her in the kitchen talking with the caterer right before I came downstairs," Donny added.

"Don't worry, you'll meet her," Zack said to Luke. "Then you'll see why I've been going on and on about her. Mom," Zack spotted his mother across the room, "can you find Jada for me?" She nodded and disappeared into the crowd.

"If you're free tomorrow, have Zack bring you over to the Jenkins' for Sunday brunch," Craig said. "There's a couple of Jenkins' here tonight, but tomorrow you'll be able to meet all of the *female* cousins who work for Jenkins & Sons Construction."

Donny gripped Luke's shoulder. "And you've never seen a bunch of *fine* ass women until you've seen them. Man, I'm talking downright gorgeous."

"So we have Craig, who's married to one of them. Zack is crazy in love with another one. What about you?" Luke directed his attention to Donny. "Are you involved or interested in either of them?"

Donny shook his head. "Nah man, I'm a one woman man and Sabrina has my heart."

Zack caught sight of Jada and Christina coming down the stairs. He wondered if years from now if his heart would still beat double time whenever she walked into the room like it was doing right then. *Damn I love this woman*. She still hadn't agreed to move in with him, but at least he got to see her practically every day.

"Hey ladies, I want to introduce you to a good friend," Zack said. He wrapped his arm around Jada's shoulder. "Sweetheart this is Luke Hayden, a friend of mine from college who is visiting right now, but might be moving here in the near future."

"Nice to meet you." Jada shook his hand. "And this is my cousin, Christina."

Zack tried to hide his smile when he noticed his friend thoroughly checking Christina out. They shook hands, but Luke still hadn't released hers. Zack couldn't blame the guy. Jada had had the same effect on him months ago, and since then he hadn't been the same.

"Well, I'm going to find my beautiful wife so that we can head out," Craig said, bumping fists with Zack. "I'll see you guys tomorrow."

"Wait up, Craig. I'm heading out too." Donny gave Zack a fist bump and hugged Jada. He waved at Luke and Christina, who were already deep in conversation.

"Come with me." Zack pulled Jada toward the bathroom, ignoring her protests. Once inside he closed and locked the door. "Okay, I'm ready for one of my birthday presents."

"Here? Right now?" Jada laughed as he backed her up against the door. "By the way, how do you know you have more than one gift?"

"Because you said presents with a 's'."

She smirked. "Figures you'd catch that." She moaned and held onto to his biceps when he nuzzled the sensitive spot behind her ear and placed kisses down her neck. "If I give you one of your gifts now, then you'll probably kick everyone out before they're ready to leave. And *then* you'll insist on your other presents. So, I think not." She weakly pushed against him.

"Ah, so there *is* more than one present," he mumbled against her shoulder blade, his hands moving slowly down her body until he reached the hidden snap keeping her dress closed. Lifting his head, Zack took a small step back and unwrapped the present he knew would be his favorite. He opened her wrap dress. His breath hitched and his heart hammered against his chest when his gaze traveled down the length of her luscious body. *Good Lord*. Her perky breasts were bare and the only garment she had on underneath was the sexiest garter belt he'd ever seen holding up her thigh-high nylons.

Happy birthday to me.

Jada pouted, her hands on her hips forced her breasts to jut out more. "You've just ruined one of your birthday surprises."

He could barely speak from the dryness in his mouth. "How do you figure that?" He dug a condom out of his wallet, unable to peel his gaze from her curvy body. She had no idea how hard she was making him. "You've been walking around this party with nothing on but a garter belt and nylons. Damn, baby. You are the best birthday present I've ever received. Had I known you were hiding all of this, we would've been in here hours ago."

Jada rolled her eyes, but he wasn't fooled by her mock disappointment. She wanted this impromptu tryst as much as he did. Otherwise, she wouldn't be still standing there with her goodies on display.

Zack felt like a kid in a candy store with all of his favorite treats vying for his attention. "I'm just trying to figure out where I'll start." But his gaze kept drifting to the black, lacy garter belt holding up her thigh-high nylons enhancing the "V" between her thighs.

"Lose the dress, sweetheart." She hesitated for a moment, but then pushed away from the door and allowed the soft material to slowly slide down her body and tumble to the floor. "My God, woman, you're absolutely breathtaking."

***

Jada had never been shy about her body and felt comfortable in the nude, especially with the way Zack perused her body. In trying to decide the perfect birthday gift, she had come up with the commando idea at the last minute. Good thing too. Never had a man made her feel so sexy and desirable. All night she wondered what he would think, but his reaction turned out better than she could have imagined. Watching him, watch her with his mouth open and his eyes brimming with desire, priceless.

Zack stepped back and hurried out of his shirt and pants, leaving them in a heap in the middle of the floor. The man was perfection with or without clothing. His hard, muscular body demanded her attention and her gaze automatically gravitated to his erection. Liquid heat soared through her body and settled between her thighs as he slowly, torturously took his time rolling on the condom.

"Normally I like to take things slow when it comes to you." He backed her up against a wall. "But the way you're looking in that garter belt, those silky nylons and those sexy ass shoes…." His words trailed off, and his mouth covered hers in a deep, hunger-filled kiss. She gripped his shoulders, fearing that her legs wouldn't hold her up with the way his tongue plunged in and out of her mouth. His kiss grew more demanding while his hard body grinded against hers.

"Mmm, I want you so bad," he growled, showering kisses on her cheek, along her jawline and down her neck.

A whimper escaped Jada's throat when he nudged her thighs apart, and his hand glided over her sex, his thumb teasing her clit. A burning desire flooded her body, and her knees trembled when he increased the pressure.

"You like that?" He nipped at her bottom lip.

"Yes," she said breathlessly, her mind swirling from the pleasure.

With the precision of a sharpshooter, Zack slipped his finger inside her opening, and Jada's breath caught when he slid in a second one. Stomach quivering, she clenched her thighs around his hand as she dug her nails into his shoulders. Pulse pounding, she caught the rhythm of his hand and moved with him, the sweet torment he inflicting was almost unbearable.

She would never get enough of him. Every day, sex with him got more intense, more adventurous. She groaned his name. His nimble fingers circled her inner core, gliding in and out of her slick heat. Taunting. Teasing. Torturing her with masterful strokes, he increased his speed. Her breaths grew labored as the pressure built. She held on tighter. Her moves grew jerky, and as if sensing her release, Zack covered her mouth with his, smothering the scream of his name from her lips. A dizzying wave of pleasure seized her, and she jerked against his hand when everything within her exploded into a thousand little pieces.

"Zack," she cried, wilting against him, unable to stop the aftershocks from overpowering her body. But before she could catch her breath, he hoisted her into his arms. Her legs automatically went around his waist and without preamble, he buried himself deep inside her.

"Oh yeah," he growled and moved her up and down on his length. "That's it, baby." He picked up speed. Harder and faster, he was relentless, his length growing thicker as he went deeper. Jada gripped the back of his short hair, her eyes closed as she hung on for the ride. Teetering on the edge herself, she knew Zack wasn't far behind. As the pressure within her grew, she squeezed her thighs together, her interior walls holding him, clutching him, pulling him in deeper until he exploded inside her.

He held her tight, bracing her between him and the wall as they collapsed against each other. Neither could speak. Heavy breaths were the only sound inside the bathroom. *Oh crap, the bathroom!* Horrified that someone might have heard them she released a low groan and dropped her head onto Zack's shoulder.

"That was the best present ever," he panted against her neck.

Men.

CHAPTER FIFTEEN

Jada couldn't remember the last time she invited a guy to Sunday brunch. For the Jenkins Family, Sunday brunch was a big deal. Not only was it a time that the whole family came together, but if you were invited to attend, you were considered family.

Jada also couldn't ever remember being so nervous waiting for one of her guests to show up. Spending the night and making love to Zack every day had her walking around in lalaland.

"Did Zack say when he and Craig would be here?" Toni asked as she carried a glass dish loaded with smothered sweet potatoes to the counter closest to the pantry. At almost seven months pregnant, she looked as if she were carrying a basketball under her T-shirt.

"They left ten minutes ago. So I think they should be here soon." Jada blocked Toni's path, stopping her midstride as Toni carried a pan of dinner rolls to the designated counter. "Didn't Gramma tell you to sit down somewhere and let us do this?"

Toni glared at her. "I'm pregnant not helpless, so move."

"And you're evil," Jada mumbled and moved to the

refrigerator to grab a couple of two-liter bottles of white soda. Before pregnancy, even if she did rope Jada into some of her shenanigans, her cousin was one of the fun ones. Now that Toni was married to Craig, a police detective, they didn't get into as much trouble. Her pregnancy probably had a lot to do with that fact too.

Jada glanced at the clock on the microwave. Zack had called to check in with her and make sure that it was still okay for his friend from New York to attend. Her grandparents loved entertaining and felt the more the merrier. She'd waited all season to invite Zack over and finally his team had a bye-week, giving the players four days in a row off.

"Jada, your man is here," Peyton announced glancing out the window over the sink.

Christina stood at the window next to Peyton but quickly moved away. "I didn't know Zack was bringing his friend." She ran her hands feverishly through her large mass of curls. "How do I look?" She turned to her sister.

Peyton stared at her and frowned. "Why do you care? Do you know him?"

"I met him last night." She smoothed out her salmon color chiffon top. "He seems like a nice guy."

"Well, I guess he must be if you're checking and rechecking yourself," Peyton said and took another look out the window.

"And it doesn't hurt that the brother is *fine*!" Toni chimed in, still moving dishes around.

Jada decided to help Toni move some of the dishes. "Luke is a friend of theirs from New York. I think Zack said he's a lawyer. He's visiting for a few days and might be moving to Cincinnati."

"Why would anyone leave New York to come to Cincinnati?" Martina strolled into the kitchen. "I know it's crazy expensive to live there, but still."

"Well, when he comes in, you can ask him." Peyton dried

her hands and went to the refrigerator. Pulling out the bowl of potato salad, she set it on the counter and then handed a huge tossed salad to Martina.

"Oh and Jada, Gramma said that you, CJ and Auntie Kay have clean up duty."

"What?" Jada didn't miss the gleam in Martina's eye or the smirk on her face.

"Hey, I'm just the messenger. I don't know what you two did, but I bet I won't be nowhere near this kitchen after everyone eats."

Jada's breath caught when Zack strolled into the room carrying three bags of ice. Even after several months, just the sight of him did wicked things to her. And when he smiled, flashing those sexy dimples, he took her breath away.

Peyton directed him and Craig to the extra coolers near the door that led to the garage.

"Hey sweetheart," Zack said pulling her into his arms. "I've missed you." Jada wrapped her arms around his neck, loving the feel of his hard, muscular body against hers. He brushed a tender kiss against her cheek before claiming her mouth.

"Hi," she mumbled against his lips. "I've missed you too."

"Ahem." Someone cleared their throat. Jada wasn't sure who, but she slowly pulled away. Zack kept one arm around her back.

Zack introduced Luke to Peyton, while Craig ushered Toni out of the kitchen. Luke shook Peyton's hand and then turned to Christina. It was clear to anyone in the room watching that something sensuous transferred between the two. Jada also didn't miss the way Christina smiled shyly at the handsome man, who was definitely her cousin's type. Dark skin, hair cut low with a little scruff on his jaw and chin. He was tall with a look that said he probably grew up on the streets, but some serious education had knocked the edge off of him. Christina always went for the intelligent, bad boy types.

They all stood around talking in the large kitchen as other family members filtered in and out preparing their plates. With over five thousand square feet of space, there was plenty of room in her grandparent's mini-mansion for everyone.

An hour into the brunch and Jada was ready to leave so she could be with Zack. Now that she'd had a taste of what it would be like to wake up in his arms, there was no other place she'd rather be. What started as a goal to find a wealthy man to provide her with the type of life that she'd always dreamed of, had turned into so much more.

"If you keep looking at me like that, I'm going to throw you over my shoulders and find an empty bedroom … or bathroom." Zack's deep voice penetrated her thoughts. When she didn't respond, unable to because of the fantasy those few words created, he placed his hand at the small of her back. "What's wrong?" Standing closer, shielding her from the others in the room. "Did something happen?"

She shook her head. When he spoke against her ear, his arm around her now, she couldn't help but remember his hard body pressed against hers in the bathroom the night before.

"I'm fine," she croaked and cleared her throat.

"You don't look fine. Do you need something to drink?"

"A glass of white wine would be good." Actually, a shot of Tequila would have been better, but she kept that to herself.

Sunday brunch was as lively as usual with the men watching football and the women discussing the latest reality shows. Occasionally Jada checked on Zack, stole a kiss, and roamed around the house to see if anyone needed anything. Her heart sang with delight during family times. Especially, when everyone was eating, laughing, and having a good time. Too often, she took her family for granted, but there were times like now that she felt blessed to be a Jenkins.

Hours later Jada and Martina washed the pots and pans that weren't able to fit in the dishwasher.

"Okay, so what gives? Why are you helping in here when you had clean up duty last week?" she asked Martina. "Just so you know, I'm not paying you this time. The last time I did, you half did the job, and I had clean up duty for two Sundays straight."

Martina laughed, which unnerved Jada. Normally her cousin had something smart to say. "Don't trip. You don't owe me anything, this time."

"Why? You don't just do stuff for me out of the goodness of your heart. I know it's going to cost me one way or the other."

"Would you relax? Your debt has been paid."

Jada dropped her hand in the dishwater, not caring that some of the water splashed on her apron. "You can't pay a debt I don't have, MJ! So what are you talking about?"

"Your boyfriend promised me two tickets to the Cincinnati and Bears game in a couple of weeks."

"Why?"

"Well, I guess I might have asked for the tickets."

"MJ!"

"Keep it down." She shoved Jada, almost causing her to lose her balance. "He said I can have the tickets under two conditions. One, I fill in for Christina and help you clean up so that she can hang out with his friend, Luke. And two, you have to attend the football game with me." Martina grabbed the dishtowel and wiped down the counter around the sink.

Jada stared at her cousin, unable to keep the smirk from spreading across her lips. "Ahh, so you need me, again."

"Come on, JJ. You know I'm not too proud to beg, but you need to think about this."

"Why? There's nothing in it for me. You know I don't want to sit out in thirty- degree weather watching grown men run up and down the field, trying to knock the crap out of each other."

"Do it for Zack."

"I don't understand."

"Girl, do I have to explain everything to you?" Martina put her hands on her hips. "He wants you to go to one of his games. If the rumors about him retiring after this season are true, then he's not going to have many more games left. You need to attend at least one of them. Might as well be the one, I'll be at." She flashed Jada one of her goofy smiles.

Zack had asked Jada before if she wanted to attend a couple of his games, but he never made it seem like a big deal whether she agreed to attend or not. So she never did.

"MJ, your mom is looking for you." Kirsten, Jada's mother, walked in with a large trash bag and sat it near the door that led out to the garage. "She said she's ready to go."

"And she said that she's ready to go – now." Katherine Jenkins, their grandmother, added when she entered the kitchen with two glass pitchers.

"I can't wait until she gets her car fixed," Martina grumbled. She turned back to Jada. "The game is in a couple of weeks. Are you in?" Jada nodded. If Zack wanted her there, she'd be there. "Cool! I'll give you the exact date soon. I'm sure you're going to want to start picking out the *perfect* outfit." Jada shot the dishtowel at her and stuck out her tongue.

"When are you two going to grow up?" Their grandmother shook her head and set the pitchers down.

"So Mama Jenkins, did Jada tell you that she's moving in with her new boyfriend?" Kirsten asked when they were the only three left in the kitchen.

Jada wanted to find the nearest dumpster to hide behind when her grandmother raised an inquiring eyebrow. Apparently, Kirsten Jenkins wasn't done with expressing her disapproval. All evening Jada had found her mother eyeing her and Zack.

"No, actually I haven't had a chance to chat with my baby lately." Jada smiled when her grandmother bumped hips with her, clearly trying to ease some of the tension between Jada and her mother.

There was always something so calming about being in her grandmother's presence, which was probably why most of the family members confided in her. Jada still hadn't made a decision about moving in with Zack, but she wanted to. She wanted to wake up to him every morning and fall asleep in his arms every night.

"I'll go and check the rest of the house and make sure there are no plates and glasses lying around. Maybe you'll be able to talk some sense into your granddaughter." Kirsten left Jada and her grandmother alone.

"Your young man seems to be very nice." Her grandmother prompted. "Tell me his name again."

"Zack, Zachary Anderson." Jada dried her hands on a dry towel and laid it on the counter. "I met him at Toni and Craig's wedding reception." The last three months had gone by so fast.

"I remember seeing the two of you dancing. I'm surprised you hadn't invited him to Sunday brunch before today."

"I did. Playing professional football doesn't allow for many Sundays off. Today is his first Sunday off since we've been dating."

"Well, I'm glad he made it today." Her grandmother grabbed a Tupperware container from out of a cabinet. "He seems quite taken with you. Even when your dad and uncles were talking to him about football today, his gaze followed you around the room."

A smile played around Jada's lips. She had to admit that Zack was very attentive, and she loved the attention.

"And by that smile on your face, I'd say the feelings are mutual."

Jada lowered her head, remembering that Katherine Jenkins didn't miss anything. Her grandmother stayed on top of her family by watching and gently asking questions. She had a gift for getting everyone to share their thoughts.

"I like him … a lot." Jada giggled, unable to stop herself. "He makes me feel things I've never felt with any other man. Gramma, he makes me happy."

Her grandmother pulled two glasses from the cupboard and sat at the breakfast bar with a pitcher of ice tea. "Sit with me." She waved to the seat next to her.

Tossing her hair across her shoulder, Jada reluctantly sat down, knowing she wasn't going to like this conversation. There were advantages of having a close-knit family, but now, sitting next to her grandmother, she remembered the disadvantages.

Katherine poured them both a glass of sweet tea. "Baby, I'm glad you're happy. Zack seems like a fine young man, but I have to ask you. Are you sure your feelings for him don't have anything to do with him being a professional football player?" Her grandmother had lowered her voice, knowing that someone could walk into the kitchen at any moment. "From the time you were a little girl, you had vowed that you were going to marry someone rich."

Hearing the words that she'd spoken plenty of times, made her recognize how shallow she sounded. Not once had she vowed to fall in love with a wonderful man and live happily ever after. Her fantasies up until a few months ago only centered on money.

She fingered the diamond tennis bracelet, which was a part of the surprise wardrobe that Zack had given her. "I've changed, Gramma. I realize now how superficial my attitude used to be. Zack is so much more than a means to an end. He's a wonderful man, who treats me like I'm a gift from God."

"You are a gift from God," her grandmother said simply, "and he should be treating you as such."

"And he does."

"Is that why you're moving in with him?"

"I never said I was moving in with him. I told Mom that he asked me, but I never said I would."

"But you're thinking about it."

Jada didn't respond. Of course, she was thinking about moving in with him. Who wouldn't? He was every woman's dream. He made her feel things she had never felt before. It didn't hurt that he could provide her with the type of life she had always imagined. Most importantly, he loved her.

"And have you thought about the challenges that come with dating someone outside of your race? Zack might be a nice man, but not everyone is ready to see a black woman with a white man."

Jada wondered if her grandmother knew that interracial couples weren't something new. "Zack and I have been dating for over three months. Sure some people stare, but for the most part, we haven't had any trouble."

Her grandmother patted her hand and smiled. "I'm glad to hear that."

"Gramma, Zack means the world to me. I would love him no matter his ethnic background and even if he didn't have money." Butterflies bounced around in her stomach just thinking about how much she loved that man.

"Love?"

"Yes, ma'am, I love him with all of my heart. I know you don't—"

"Baby," her grandmother grabbed hold of her hand and squeezed, "I think it's wonderful that you're in love. I have to tell you, I never thought I'd hear those words coming from you."

"I know. I guess I'm finally growing up." Jada smiled at her grandmother who wrapped her arm around Jada's shoulder and placed a kiss against her temple. "Though I've always wanted to get married and have a fairytale life, I never thought I'd fall in love with anyone." *Or anyone else.* Her family knew Dion existed, but didn't know the extent of their relationship or how he treated her toward the end. "Zack is … I can't even find the words that would describe how breathless he leaves me."

"Then why just move in with him? Why not marry him?"

Silence fell between them. Jada knew Zack was looking to get married and settle down one day, but he hadn't said anything specifically about marrying her.

***

"Are you sure you don't want to go home with me?" Zack asked Jada as he drove toward the house she shared with Christina.

"I would love to go home with you, but I have to get up pretty early for work tomorrow. It would be better if I went home tonight."

They road in silence and normally it wouldn't be a big deal, but Zack had a feeling something else was going on. Whereas she was laughing and joking while at her grandparents' house, she now seemed a little sad.

He reached for her hand, linking his fingers with hers. "Tell me what's wrong." When she opened her mouth as if to deny anything was wrong, he stopped her. "Don't bother saying nothing, because I know you. There's something on your mind so talk to me. Sweetheart, tell me what's going on."

After some persuading, she told him about her conversation with her mother weeks ago and then today with her grandmother. Jada never came across as a person who let others dictate what she did, but Zack could see how much their opinion mattered to her. He had to admit that if he had a daughter, he would be concerned about her moving in with some guy too.

"Zack, it's not that I don't love you because I do." She squeezed his hand. "But I can't move in with you."

Zack brought her hand up to his mouth and kissed the back of it without taking his eyes off the road. "Are you basing your decision on your family's opinion, or is this truly your decision?"

Zack pulled up to Christina's house and cut off the engine. Disappointment churned inside his chest. When he was engaged to Leslie, he thought he was in love, but the feelings he had for Jada far exceeded anything he had ever felt for any woman.

Jada glanced down at their joined hands. "When I was a little girl, I always dreamed of getting married. I imagined walking down the aisle wearing a long flowing champagne color dress in a huge castle," she said excitement painting every word. "Talking with my grandmother tonight, I was reminded of that fantasy." Jada finally looked at him. "Zack you are an amazing man who I absolutely adore, but moving in with you is not enough for me. I want the fantasy."

And he wanted her to have the fantasy. "Then marry me."

CHAPTER SIXTEEN

Jada slid the metal "s" slip onto the ductwork and connected the corner piece to the eight-foot joint already hanging from the ceiling. Wiping sweat from her forehead with the sleeve of her shirt, she gripped the top of the ladder and released an exhausted sigh.

"You okay Your Highness?" Nick asked, using the nickname she hadn't heard in weeks. He worked at the other end of the duct run they were hanging. "You've been going at it pretty hard these last few days."

Working helped keep her mind off Zack and his impromptu proposal five days earlier. She couldn't believe he was serious about marrying her, offering her everything she had ever wanted. Yet she wasn't ready to accept his proposal.

"Yeah, I'm fine. I'm just ready to get this job done so that we can start the Sanford project next week." She climbed down from the eight-foot ladder and moved it over in order to attach a hanger around the ductwork Nick had just hung.

"How's it going with you and Zack? You haven't mentioned him lately."

She hadn't seen Zack in days, not since the Sunday

brunch. They talked every day, but his practice schedule had changed for the week and Jada used the excuse of exhaustion to keep from driving all the way out to his house. Prior to the brunch, she'd spend a few nights during the week at his place, as well as Sunday nights after his home games. When she spoke with him earlier, he had mentioned how much he missed her, telling her that if she didn't come to him, then he would be at her place by the time she got off of work.

"Jada?"

"Huh?" Nick's voice brought her back to the present. She hadn't noticed him standing nearby until she felt a slight bump to her ladder.

"Come on down."

"I'm not finished attaching this hanger."

"I'll take care of it." He held the ladder while she climbed down. "We don't need you falling off the damn ladder while you're off in la-la land. What's going on with you? I asked how Zack was, and it's like you zoned out, staring off into space."

"I don't know." Jada put her hammer and screwdriver back into her tool belt that was sitting on the floor near the ladder. "I have a lot on my mind. Oh and Zack is fine. Actually he's better than fine. He's wonderful." Her voice trailed off. She hadn't told anyone about Zack's suggestion that they get married. She planned to keep the proposal to herself until she worked out some things in her head.

"If he's so wonderful, why do you look as if you've lost your best friend?"

She wasn't totally sure. All she knew is that since he mentioned marriage, fear had settled into her soul. Yes, she wanted to get married, and she couldn't imagine being with anyone other than Zack. Yet, she knew Zack had the ability to break her heart, and she didn't know if she wanted to take the risk. Getting married to someone wealthy had always been her goal, but Zack had a power over her that made her uncomfortable. She was used to being in control when she dated. Somehow he had managed to knock down the barriers she had built to protect her heart.

"See this is why I will never get serious with a woman and settle down." Nick said and folded the ladder, carrying it to the corner that held much of their equipment for the job. "People fall in love and then start walking around in a daze. Who has time for that crap?"

Jada laughed. "It's not crap. It's a beautiful feeling." Or so she kept telling herself.

***

Later that evening, Jada pulled onto Zack's magnificent property, glad to have made the trip in one piece. The city had finally gotten the snow that the forecasters warned them about for the past two days. Growing up in Ohio, she knew how to drive in snow, but tonight, tired and hungry, she only wanted to eat and go to bed. Her nerves and patience were on edge, and she was happy to be home.

Home.

Though she hadn't agreed to move in with Zack, considering the amount of time she spent at his place, it was starting to feel a little like home.

She pulled through the gate surrounding his estate and followed the circular drive around to the main house, not stopping until she reached the outdoor water fountain, the focal point of the front yard. The traditional brick home made her and Christina's place look like a gingerbread house. Despite having a luxury loft near the stadium, he spent most of his time at this location, appreciating the privacy.

Jada shut off her car, lifted the hood of her jacket over her head, and eased out of the vehicle, careful not to slip on the snow accumulating on the ground. It wasn't until she activated the car locks that she noticed the small pick-up truck that she didn't recognize, parked on the side of the house near the garage.

A shiver gripped her body when a blast of wind pushed

her toward the front entrance. *Brrr*. Zack had once mentioned spending his winters in Los Angeles once he retired. Right now, the idea of leaving the harsh winters of Ohio was starting to appeal to her.

Jada entered through the front door with the key that Zack had given her a few days before his birthday. The moment she stepped across the threshold, she heard yelling.

What the heck is going on?

She stood planted in the wide foyer, debating on whether to walk farther into the house. Hearing the voices grow louder and fearing for Zack's safety, she followed the yelling to the library.

"What do you mean I can't move in here? You have more than enough space, and it's only for three or four months."

Jada folded her lower lip between her teeth as she stood in the hall outside the library. She could see Zack and his brother, Shane, facing off, mere inches between them. They were both around the same height, but Zack had about thirty pounds on his brother. Shane scowled. Jada knew the scene could get a lot worse before it got better.

"Shane, I'm not running some hotel where you can just get a room whenever you want. It's time I make some changes as far as you and I are concerned. I'm not a bank that you can get money from whenever you decide to quit a job. You can't stroll in and out of my home at your leisure, and if I ever let you use any of my vehicles in the future, I expect you to at least replace the gasoline."

"Are you kidding me? You have all of this," he lifted his arms out and turned in a circle, "and it's not like you're hurting for money. Yet you're trippin' because I need a little help every now and then."

Jada listened on, unable to pull herself away from the door. Zack was the most generous person she'd ever met. He wouldn't pull his support from his brother if he didn't have a good reason.

"Hell, every now and then?" Zack glared at his brother.

"Shane you have your hand out every other month. It's not like you're asking for twenty or thirty bucks when you come to me, it's more like a hundred here, five hundred there. I'm sick of your mess. Just because I have a few bucks in my pocket don't mean that I'm trying to give it all away. I work damn hard for everything I have, and if you held on to a job for more than a week, maybe you could get yourself together."

"So it's like that, huh? You gon' just cut me off? We're supposed to be family, and this is how you do me?" Shane pointed at himself. "I shouldn't have to pay money back to you. You should be willing to just give it to—"

"You know what, Shane? You need to go. Jada will be here shortly, and I don't want her coming home to your shit."

"That's what this is about isn't it?" Shane yelled. "Ever since you hooked up with that—."

"That what?" Zack spat the two words out with a lethal ease that Jada had never heard from him. "That what, Shane? Go ahead and say it so I can kick your ass right now."

"You've changed." Shane took a few steps back, and Jada released the breath she didn't know she was holding. Zack looked like a bull ready to charge, and there was no telling what he would've done to Shane had they not put some space between them.

"You're damn right I've changed. That woman who you seem to have a problem with is the best thing that has ever happened to me. Instead of you wishing me well and welcoming her to our family, you've been treating her like a second-class citizen."

"She's not good enough for you! Man, don't you see that? You're so concerned about me using you, what about her? I'm sure by now she's asked you to pay her bills and buy her a new car."

"Unlike you, she hasn't asked me for a damn thing!"

"Oh, well I'm sure she will. But tell me something. How

do you go from dating supermodel-type women to hooking up with a construction worker?" Shane shook his head. "I'm sure you can do better."

"You of all people are going to look down on someone because of the type of work they do? You can't even hold a job for more than a few months. How crazy do you sound right now?"

The heaviness in Jada's heart felt like a two-ton boulder. Did the rest of his family feel the same way? Did they all think that she wasn't good enough for Zack? According to her father, she came out of the womb self-confident as if she were the princess of power, the most powerful woman in the universe. But then Dion knocked her down a peg or two, telling her that she wouldn't have been good enough for him even if he weren't already married. Did Zack and his family feel the same way? The possibility wedged in her gut like a steel weight, anchored to one of her vital organs.

She staggered backwards until she bumped the wall, but couldn't get her feet to keep moving. She should've been running out of that house, getting as far away from Zack as she could, yet, her heart wouldn't let her leave.

"You are a multi-millionaire scraping the bottom of the barrel." Shane continued, disgust in his tone. "Has it really come to this? Can't you find someone in your tax bracket? You have to settle for—"

Zack grabbed his brother by the front of his jacket. "Get out!" he roared. "Get the hell out of my house, now! As a matter of fact, we're done. Don't call me. Don't come by my house. Hell, act as if you don't even know me." Zack pushed him away, not seeming to care that Shane tripped over an ottoman though he righted himself immediately. "We're done. Get out!"

A stab of guilt lodged in Jada's chest. The last thing she wanted was to come between him and his brother. Family meant everything to her. There was no way she would be the reason for dissention in anyone's family.

167

Willing herself to move, she took a step forward, but stopped when Zack's gaze met hers.

"Jada," he said, barely loud enough for her to hear him.

"Oh great! If it isn't the gold-digging, walking Barbie doll."

Before Jada could move or say anything, Zack charged at his brother like he was a defensive tackle, rushing the passer. He grabbed the front of his brother's jacket and slammed him to the floor, then raised his fist sending a punch after punch to Shane's face. His brother fought back, landing a few punches of his own.

Oh no.

"Stop!" Jada screamed, running toward them. "Please, Zack, don't! Don't do this! Please, baby, stop!"

"Get up!" Zack lifted his brother and dragged him out of the room, despite Shane fighting him.

Jada swiped at the tears that were beginning to fall, and her heart pounded in her chest.

Zack walked back into the room but stayed near the door staring at her. With the sleeve of his long sleeved T-shirt, he wiped the blood from his lip. Jada didn't move from her position near the sofa. She didn't know what to say or what to do. Part of her wanted to apologize for causing a rift between him and his brother, but the other part of her was glad he had defended her honor.

"Sweetheart, I'm sorry you had to hear all of that." He eased toward her, but the confidence he normally displayed was missing. Jada figured it was due to not knowing what she was thinking or how she would respond to him. "Shane is a very angry and selfish person. He has been that way since our father walked out years ago. Ignore anything you heard him say."

Jada swallowed hard when his hand touched her shoulder and then slid down her arm until he grabbed hold of her hand, tenderness sparkling in his crystal blue eyes. She willed herself not to cry, but couldn't help it when a few tears slipped through and crept down her cheek. Deep in her heart, she knew she was good enough for any man, but she couldn't seem to shake Shane's words. Zack had accomplished so much in his life, while she had nothing to show for her life but a boat-load of debt.

Zack pulled her into his arms and held her tight. "I'm sorry." Jada's head rested against his chest, his heart pounding loudly against her ear. The love she felt being in his arms should have been enough to soothe the ache in her heart, but it wasn't.

"I think I should go." She pulled away slightly, but he prevented her from moving much with the gentle hold he had on her upper arms.

"I can't let you leave. Not like this. Not without us talking about what just happened."

She shook her head. "I can't do this right now." She eased out of his hold and headed to the door.

"Jada."

She stopped and glanced at him over her shoulder. If she stayed, she would never leave and right now she had to go someplace and clear her head.

CHAPTER SEVENTEEN

"You know you played like shit out there today, don't you?" Coach James said from behind his desk, leaning forward in his office chair. "In all of the years I've coached you, you have always brought your "A" game. I don't know what's going on, but it has to stop. The team needs you." Zack lowered his gaze to the top of the oak desk, tension twisting in his gut like a spring waiting to pop loose. "There are two more games left, Chicago and Denver. We need you out there giving your best. If all of you guys show up to play, then I think we can pull out some wins."

At that moment, Zack didn't give a damn about football or anything else. He could only think of Jada. He hadn't seen her in almost two weeks. Every effort he made to talk to her, or see her came up empty. Stopping by Jenkins & Sons twice didn't help. Peyton wanted to help him, but couldn't give him Jada's location for fear of drama breaking out. When Zack sought Christina's help, she let him wait for Jada one evening at their house, but Jada never showed. Instead, she spent that night at her parent's place.

"Zack?"

He looked up to find his coach observing him with

concern. "Sorry coach." Zack ran his hands through his damp hair. "I'll be ready next week."

Coach James's forehead wrinkled. "I'm not sure what's going on, but I hope you know that if you need me for anything, all you have to do is ask."

Zack nodded. "I know. Thanks." Zack slunk out of the building, his body engulfed in tides of weariness. Something had to give. He either needed to find a way to connect with Jada to find out what was on her mind or move on with his life.

An hour later, Zack pulled up to his mother's house. He had purchased the three-bedroom, two-bath bungalow with his first signing check. Buying things to make her life easier and more enjoyable gave him a sense of accomplishment. His mother's love and support never wavered. When he was growing up, she refused to let him give up on his dreams, and there was nothing he wouldn't do for her. He even accepted that she wanted to marry an immigrant she didn't love in order to help him stay in the country.

Zack climbed out of his truck and strolled up the walkway. The door had swung open before he had a chance to ring the doorbell.

"Hi, son. Come on in."

"Hey, Mom, something smells good in here." He shrugged out of his jacket, trying to ignore the throbbing in his shoulders and back. Feeling like he had been run over by a Mack truck wasn't uncommon after a game, but today was worse. He had taken a beating on the field and skipped the Jacuzzi soak and massage he usually received after a game. Zack knew his pain was from a combination of getting pounded by three-hundred pound men, and the fact that he couldn't get Jada off his mind.

"I made your favorite, honey."

The savory scent of basil and garlic drew him to the all-white kitchen with top of the line appliances and plenty of granite counter space. The kitchen was his mother's favorite room in the house, and she could always be found in there whipping up something delicious.

He inhaled deeply, and his mouth watered. Ms. Mal's lasagna was amazing, but no one could top his mother's.

"Shane stopped by yesterday," his mother said.

Zack didn't respond and kept eating. Shane could fall off the face of the earth for all he cared.

"He mentioned that you had lost your mind and that I should see about getting you some help."

Zack's fork stopped mid-air. His gaze darted to his mother. He didn't miss her raised eyebrow, and her lips twitching as if trying to keep from laughing.

Zack shoved the fork full of food into his mouth and shook his head. If anyone needed mental help, it was Shane. As kids, their relationship had its moments of drama, but in the last ten or fifteen years, they barely tolerated each other.

"So what? No comment? Your brother calls you crazy and you have nothing to say."

"Nope, except this lasagna is good as usual. I bet with a good marketing campaign, you could make a killing selling this by the pan."

"I'm glad you're enjoying it. Maybe I'll give Jada the recipe so she can make it for you sometime." Zack knew his mother was baiting him, but he didn't stop by to talk about Jada. Yet, he knew he needed to talk to someone.

"So, what do you know ... about Jada and me?"

"I know the TV sports broadcasters have been criticizing you more than usual. They say you haven't played too good the last couple of games. I also know you're not looking well. Clearly, you haven't been sleeping. And I know you haven't mentioned Jada not once in the past thirty minutes, which is a first since you met her."

She turned from him and went back to washing dishes. His mother had a sixth sense when it came to knowing something was wrong with any of her children. *That's probably why she called and invited me to dinner.*

172

"Jada is avoiding me." Zack laid his fork down and wiped his mouth. He propped his elbows on the breakfast bar and rested his head in his hands. He was beyond tired but didn't look forward to going home to an empty house.

His mother dried her hands and stood on the other side of the breakfast bar facing Zack. "Why do I have a feeling your oldest brother has something to do with this new development?"

Zack replayed the events of the night Shane was at his house and the words that were spoken. The more he thought about the hurt on Jada's face, the angrier Zack became. He couldn't help but wonder if he could've done or said something more. If he had known that when she walked out of his door that she was walking out of his life, he would have begged her to stay.

"I had to cut Shane out of my life. I can't have him disrespecting the woman I love. The woman I want to marry one day."

"Growing up as an only child, I had always wanted my children to be each other's best friend." His mother's voice held a hint of sadness. "I'm not sure where I went wrong with Shane. Even as a child there were times he was angry at the world, and then there were other times he made me proud to be his mother. I don't know what happened. I often wondered if your father had stayed around if Shane would've turned out differently."

Raised by her grandmother, his mother was deprived of love, friends, and any freedom until she was nineteen. It wasn't until her grandmother died that she had a chance to live a little. Zack toyed with the handle of his fork. He remembered her telling him that she married their father within two months of meeting him and became pregnant soon after. The marriage ended when she was three months pregnant with Zack's youngest brother and left to raise four children by herself.

"I understand why you're distancing yourself from

Shane. I hate you two couldn't work out your differences, but let me give you something to think about. Shane drives you nuts, and I get that. But, honey, you have to understand. Your brother has had a tough few years and hasn't always made the best choices."

"And that's my fault?"

"I'm not saying it's your fault. What I'm saying is that everything doesn't come as easy to others as it might come for you."

"Mom, I have worked hard for everything I've accomplished. If Shane applied himself maybe he could stop getting himself into jams and hold onto a job."

His mother reached across the counter and squeezed his arm. "Honey, I'm proud of all of your accomplishments, but just because Shane hasn't had some of the same successes as you, doesn't mean he hasn't been trying. Some people have made poor choices that have taken their lives in the wrong direction. That doesn't mean they're not trying, and it doesn't mean that they're not hard workers or that they're all bad people."

"What exactly are you saying?"

"Zack, you are a helper by nature. Yet when someone disappoints you, you're quick to cut them loose. You don't give people a chance to redeem themselves."

"So you're saying I should forgive Shane for using me and forget everything he said about Jada even though he hasn't apologized for anything?"

"I'm not saying that at all. I'm saying don't give up on your brother. He's family and sometimes we have to give people a second chance." Zack looked at her sideways, his eyebrow raised. His mother smiled. "Okay, or maybe we have to give them three, four or maybe even five chances."

Forgiving and giving second chances had never come easy for Zack, but maybe his mother was right.

"Think about it, honey. And as for Jada, she loves you."

"Yeah, maybe," he snorted, "but right now I need her to

talk to me."

His mother walked around the breakfast bar to where he sat. Hugging him, she said, "I think Jada is perfect for you. She's cute, sassy, and I can tell she has a good heart. I could also tell by the way she looked at you during your party that she adores you. Don't give up. She'll come around." His mother went back to washing dishes. "And if she doesn't, there's only one thing to do."

"What's that?"

"Find her and convince her that you can't live without her."

Zack finished his meal while thinking about all that his mother had said. If opportunity presented itself, maybe he would reach out to Shane, but right now Jada was at the forefront of his mind.

He stood, wiped his mouth, and carried his dishes to the sink. Kissing his mother's cheek, he said, "Thanks for dinner … and the talk."

"Anytime, dear."

His mother walked him to the door and the moment he slipped into his jacket, his cell phone vibrated. *Please let it be Jada*. He dug through his pocket and peeped at the screen.

Craig.

Zack had five missed calls and a text.

GET TO COUNTY HOSPITAL A.S.A.P.

Twenty minutes later Zack rushed through the hospital's door, his heart pounding in his ears as fear rattled around in his gut. He still didn't know why he had been summoned to the hospital since each time he tried calling Craig back, he got his voicemail. All types of thoughts ran through his mind, with Jada at the center of each scenario. If anything had happened to her…

When Zack didn't find Craig or any of the Jenkins family in the halls or waiting room, he headed to the receptionist desk.

"Zack."

He whipped around to find Craig heading in his direction.

"What the hell is going on?" Zack spat out before Craig could speak, his stomach churning with anxiety. "Please tell me nothing has happened to Jada. If…" His voice hitched.

"It's not Jada." Craig stood two feet away rubbing the back of his neck, looking everywhere but at Zack.

"Craig," Zack growled and moved closer, "so help me if you don't tell me what the fu—"

"It's Leslie."

"Leslie?" Zack leaned back and put his hands on his waist, his chest heaving as he stared at his friend wondering if Craig had lost his mind.

"Yeah. Another detective and I received a domestic violence call. Leslie happened to be the victim and was brought in a couple of hours ago. Man, she's in bad shape. Her fiancé beat her."

"And you called me because of what?"

"Let's step over here." Zack followed him to a secluded spot away from the waiting area. "Man, she has no one."

"*And*?"

Craig's greenish-hazel eyes darkened. "And I thought your ass would have some damn compassion and help her out. Her fiancé is in custody, and her brother is nowhere to be found. You know better than anyone that she has no one, and we both know that you can help her."

"Craig, what exactly are you asking me to do here?" Zack heard the leeriness in his own voice. He was sorry about whatever happened to Leslie, but her well-being was not his concern.

"Go in and see her. Talk to her. Listen to her. She can really use a friend."

"And you called *me*? Apparently you have forgotten the hell that that woman put me through. I almost lost everything because of her. Now you're asking me to be her *friend*?" Zack let out a harsh laugh and backed away. He ran his hand through his hair not believing what he was hearing. "I can't do this, Craig. I have nothing to say to her and if that makes me a jerk then, oh well."

Craig gripped Zack's shoulder and squeezed. "You forget that I know you. This jacked up uncaring attitude is not you. Listen, man, I know I'm asking a lot here, but I really think she's changed. She wants to make things right with you. Give her a chance."

Minutes later, Zack pushed open the door to Leslie's hospital room, still not comfortable with his decision to see her. Tension gnawed at the back of his neck as he stood just over the threshold and inhaled deeply. Slowly releasing the breath, he took in the soft yellow walls, the single window with the closed blinds and the bed holding the woman of his nightmares. The bandage covering the right side of her face and the cast on her left arm didn't soften his feelings toward her.

Damn, I can't do this. He stood rooted in place, flashbacks of what she'd done to him, clouded his mind.

"Zack?" Leslie's soft voice interrupted his musing.

After a moment of hesitation, he finally took a step forward. Zack had no idea what he'd say to her. What could he say? For months, the thought of her made his blood boil and seeing her not too long ago hadn't helped his feelings toward her.

"Thanks for coming," she said and pushed a button that raised the head of the bed. "I know you hate me, but I needed to see you."

Some of the anger toward her subsided, but was replaced by a sense of guilt seeing just how bad she'd been beaten. Her swollen eye and busted lip stood out like a bright neon sign.

"How?" He spoke the only word he could form, sickened that someone could do something like this to her. No one deserved to be beaten, not even her.

She started shaking her head but stopped and shrug. "He got angry and this time was worse than the times before."

"He's done this before?" Zack growled but reined in the sudden anger swirling within him. "Did you report his ass? Why didn't you stay away from him if you knew he had a problem?"

Raw hurt glittered in her eyes. "Where else was I going to go? I have no family unless you count my worthless brother," she snapped. "Zack, this is not why I wanted to see you."

"No? Then why did you ask to see me?" He braced himself for her to ask for money or worse, for them to get back together, which would never happen.

"When Craig showed up, I knew this would be my only chance to make things right with you since you wouldn't answer any of my calls. Zack, I wanted to apologize."

"For?" He knew he was acting like a jerk, but he couldn't help it.

"For everything," she huffed. "The lies, the betrayal, and everything else I did to you. I'm not the same person I was back then. I know my past is no excuse for all that I've done, but I need you to understand that I grew up with nothing. I had to hustle for everything I got and unfortunately I hurt people along the way, especially you."

Sometimes we have to give people a second chance, his mother's words darted across his mind.

"Zack, you were the best thing that ever happened to me. No one had ever treated me as kind and was as generous as you were. And going through what I went through today, I'll never forgive myself for accusing you of beating me. I can't apologize to you enough for almost ruining everything you've worked so hard for."

For the very first time, the anger that Zack felt toward Leslie wasn't there. He didn't know if he could forgive her, but he no longer wished her a life in hell. By the way she looked, she had already been there.

"I'm not sure what to say to you." Zack leaned against the wall near the side of the bed, exhaustion suddenly taking root in his body.

"Craig told me you had moved on and was seeing someone," Leslie said staring at her hands before her eyes met his. "I'm happy for you. I'm glad you didn't let what I did to you keep you from finding happiness."

So much for happiness considering Jada isn't speaking to me.

"Zack, please tell me that you can forgive me. I swear to you I'll never contact you again. All I need to know is that you forgive me."

Zack studied Leslie. Maybe Craig was right, maybe she had changed. *Or maybe we have to give them three, four or maybe even five chances*, his mother's words played around in his head.

Zack pushed away from the wall and approached the bed. "I forgive you … and I'll see what I can do to help you get back on your feet."

CHAPTER EIGHTEEN

Jada sat at her grandfather's desk, needing to be in a place that always brought her peace. Stopping by her grandparent's house for a short visit after work seemed like a good idea initially, but her whole visit had been filled with thoughts of Zack.

She spun around in the chair and faced the large window behind the desk. Staring out into the darkness, her gaze landed on the plot of land where her grandmother planted her garden each year. Jada knew she'd never be able to look at a garden, fishing equipment or Timberland boots without thinking about the last few months with Zack.

A tear slid down her cheek, and she quickly swiped it away with the back of her hand. Zack offered her everything she'd ever wanted, and she had walked away from him.

"Jada?"

She swung around in the chair at the sound of her grandfather's voice. A strip of moonlight shining through the window guided his path to the desk. At over six feet tall, with a solid build, Steven Jenkins had an impressive presence.

"What are you doing in here by yourself, and why are

you sitting in the dark?"

Jada sighed and rested her head against the high-back desk chair. "Just thinking." When she decided to hide out in her grandfather's office, a place of serenity, she hadn't bothered to turn on any of the lights.

Her grandfather flicked on the desk lamp and sat in one of the upholstered chairs in front of his desk.

"Anything you want to talk about?" He crossed his legs and interlocked his hands over his knee. "I'm a good listener."

Jada smiled. "You're the best listener." The smile slipped from her lips as she tried to zone in on her problem. "Zack asked me to marry him." She played with one of her dangling earrings as she stared down at the desk, not looking at anything in particular. "I'm not sure I can."

"Why not? Do you love him?"

"I love him very much, but I'm not sure it's enough."

"What do you mean by you're not sure if it's enough?"

"I'm not sure if I'm enough for him." She dropped her hands into her lap. "Grampa, I have nothing to offer him."

"Honey, what are you talking about? You are a sweet, smart, and amazing young woman. Any man would be lucky to have you. Did he say or do something to you?"

"Oh no, nothing like that. Zack has always been a perfect gentleman. He is the sweetest man I've ever met," she said on a sob. "He's too good for me."

Steven stood and walked around his desk and pulled her into a standing position. When he wrapped his arms around her, the tears that Jada had been holding at bay for the last couple of weeks, fell freely. "You said yourself that I only think about myself."

Her grandfather leaned back and lifted her chin with his finger, forcing her to look at him.

"When did I ever say that?"

"You said that it's not always about me."

He chuckled and pulled her back into his strong arms,

rubbing her back. Jada soaked in the love from his embrace. She didn't know what she would do without her family, especially her grandparents.

"Honey, when I said that it's not always about you, I wanted you to understand that you have to think about others sometimes. You are one of the most loving people I know, but there are times when you get on a tangent with only *Jada* in mind."

He was right, and the truth wasn't easy to hear. If only she were more like Christina and Toni, her cousins who had more compassion in their pinky fingers than she had in her whole body.

Jada pulled away from her grandfather and went to stand at the window, gazing out into the darkness. "Zack is … absolutely wonderful, Grampa. Not only is he successful on the football field, but did you know he has a degree in finance, and a MBA?" She turned to face her grandfather, folding her arms across her chest. "If that's not enough, he gives millions to charities and probably does more volunteer work in one week than I have in all of my life. Unless he needs someone to tell him the difference between a Gucci and a Versace handbag, I … I have nothing to offer him."

"Did you talk to Zack about this?"

She shook her head. She'd been avoiding him, but if she knew him as well as she thought she did, he was going to come looking for her soon.

"I can't speak for Zack, but let me tell you what I was looking for when I decided I was ready for a mate." He leaned against the corner of his desk, facing her. "I wanted someone who I could trust and depend on. Someone who would stand by me when no one else would. Jada, most men want a woman who will love and respect them. If we're lucky she can cook and enjoy some of the things we enjoy, like sports or fishing." A smile played around his lips and Jada knew he had heard about some of her horrific dates with Zack. "Honey, Zack doesn't want to marry you for

182

what you can do for him, or for what you have. He wants you to be his wife for the way you make him feel."

Her grandfather had never steered her wrong before, but could it be that simple? Could Zack love her with her flaws and all? Would he still love her if he knew she'd been on the prowl for a wealthy husband?

Forty-five minutes later, Jada dragged herself into the house she shared with Christina. All she wanted to do was take a shower and crawl into the bed. The long hours at work were finally starting to catch up to her. She hadn't had a good night's sleep since the last time she'd slept with Zack.

Zack.

She missed him so much, she physically ached.

"CJ, I'm home," Jada announced.

"Well, it's about time." Jada groaned when MJ walked out of the kitchen eating cookies and carrying a glass of milk. "I never thought I'd see the day you'd request overtime. Rumor has it, you're trying to get out of debt. Or is it that you're trying to work yourself to death?" MJ sat on the sofa and flipped through the television channels.

"Where's CJ?" Jada leaned against the sofa, too tired to stand up straight and too tired to sit down knowing that she'd eventually have to get back up.

"Here I am." CJ carried a bag of microwave popcorn and plopped down on the sofa next to MJ. "Where you been?"

"Gramma and Grampa's house."

"Oh, what did Gramma cook today?"

"Never mind that, we have important things to talk about." MJ turned slightly on the sofa to look at Jada. "Whatever is going on with you and Zack, you need to fix it. He's been playing like crap."

"MJ, I can't control how Zack plays."

"Actually, I think you can. His game didn't start going downhill until you guys had your argument, or whatever." She waved her hand. "He started fumbling and playing like a rookie about the same time you started moping around. So you need to do whatever you have to do get back together with him. Besides, where else are you going to find a man who puts up with you?"

"Oh, shut up and move over." Jada squeezed in between them on the sofa and grabbed a handful of CJ's popcorn.

"She's right, JJ. Well, in her own twisted way. If you love Zack, you're going to have to talk out whatever the problem is." She shrugged. "You love him. He loves you. Work it out and put that man out of his misery."

She knew they were right, but she wasn't ready to face Zack. Not until she had something to bring to the table.

"Don't forget you promised to go to the football game with me Sunday." MJ dunked a chocolate chip cookie into her glass of milk. "I need to double check the time."

"I'm not going." Jada rarely backed out of a commitment, but this was one she couldn't keep. Even if she didn't see Zack face-to-face, she didn't want to be anywhere near him. Just knowing they were in the same stadium would make her want to seek him out once the game was over and she couldn't. She wasn't ready.

"You have to go to that game. I told him that you would be there."

"I can't."

"Yes you can. You have to."

"Why?" Her cousin had always been persistent, but Jada had a feeling there was more to her being a pain than what she was saying.

"Because this is the second to the last game before the playoffs. They need a win. If you're not there, he's going to continue to get his butt kicked out there on the field."

Jada didn't want to believe her cousin, but Nick had told her about Zack's poor performance. She didn't see how sitting in the bleachers, freezing her butt off, would make a difference.

"Something else you might want to think about," MJ continued, "he's going up against three hundred pound linebackers. If he keeps getting hammered the way he has been, he could get seriously injured."

Jada's heart sank. She would die if something happened to Zack, especially if she were the reason. "Fine. I'll go." She stood and walked toward the stairs, more than ready to fall into her bed. Before she climbed the first step, she turned back to the living room. "Since you guys seem to be in touch with Zack. Let him know that if I'm sitting out in the cold to watch him play football, the least he can do is win."

"Tell him yourself." CJ shoved more popcorn into her mouth. "I'm sure he would love to hear from you."

Christina had covered for Jada for almost two weeks, making excuses to Zack of why she couldn't see him. She hadn't told anyone about Zack and Shane's argument, figuring that one of her brothers or cousins would hunt Zack's brother down and put a hurting on him.

MJ stood and yawned. "Yeah, JJ, tell him."

"I can't," she said, the heaviness in her chest suffocating her. "I'm not ready see or talk to him yet."

***

A week later, Zack drove toward Christina's house determined to see Jada. He thought, for sure, he would see her at the Chicago game the previous week, but she had left the moment the game was over. Tonight, he and his team had just returned to Cincinnati after losing to Denver. He knew it wasn't a good idea to show up at their house in the middle of the night, but he refused to go another day without seeing her.

Thirty minutes later, he stood outside their front door. The house was dark, but Zack couldn't turn around and leave. It had been three weeks since he had last seen her. He wasn't going another night without holding her in his arms.

He shifted from one foot to the other, leaning on the doorbell. He was sure Jada wouldn't be the one answering the door. A tornado could touch down, and she'd probably sleep through it.

Minutes later, the door swung open, and Christina stood in the doorway with a bat in her hands.

"You apparently took one too many hits in the head out there on that field today. Do you have any idea what time it is?" Her long curly hair was all over the place, and her eyes were bloodshot red.

He glanced at the Cartier watch on his wrist. "It's a little after one."

"And you thought it was okay to drop by for a visit?"

"Christina, I have to see her. I'm sorry, but I'm not leaving until I do."

She sighed and lowered the bat. "She's upstairs. Good luck waking her. She's been working ten hours a day during the week and every Saturday. So trying to wake her up, will be like trying to wake the dead."

"Okay." He started up the stairs.

"Oh, one more thing. Fix whatever is going on between you two. She's driving our family nuts."

Zack knocked before entering. His eyes adjusted to the semi-dark room where only a sliver of light from a nightlight near the bathroom shown. The metallic wall covering with black, white, and red accessories placed strategically around the room were unique but classy, like the woman occupying the elegant space.

He eased toward the queen-sized bed, ignoring the sharp pain gripping his back and his left thigh. After the game they played, he needed a good long soak to work out the kinks in his body, but that would have to wait. Right now, he wanted nothing more than to be near Jada.

His gaze traveled the length of her sleeping form. She was already petite, but she looked as if she had lost weight in the weeks they'd been apart, making her look even smaller. Watching her now, he recognized that the depth of his feelings for her were much deeper than he ever could have imagined.

He wanted to wake her, but decided to let her sleep.

Instead, he sat on a long, black and white chaise lounge near the bed, prepared to wait until she awakened. This time she wouldn't be able to run or hide.

I will do whatever it takes to prove my love for you, was his last waking thought before he drifted asleep.

CHAPTER NINETEEN

Jada hugged her pillow tighter and snuggled deeper into the soft goose down, refusing to open her eyes. She was so glad Peyton had forced her to take a day off. Otherwise, she probably would've had to call in. The long hours had finally taken a toll on her mind and body. She couldn't get out of bed even if she wanted to and today, she didn't want to.

I wonder if Zack's team won yesterday.

She released a low growl and pounded her pillow, frustrated that she couldn't go more than a few minutes without thoughts of him invading her mind. He was like an addiction. She'd had him, now she craved him more than she craved Godiva chocolates.

I miss him so much.

Jada's eyes popped open. A terrifying realization washed over her. What if Zack didn't want her anymore? What if he had already moved on?

She flipped over onto her back, kicking away the covers that were tangled around her legs. It was time to stop hiding. Her grandfather had been right. She was worthy of Zack's love. It was time she was completely honest with him. He would either accept all her flaws, or she would move on.

On a sigh, Jada turned onto her side and bolted straight up in bed. *What is he doing here?* Shocked to see Zack stretched out on her chaise lounge, her hand flew to her chest as she fought to keep her tears at bay.

He came. Just when she thought he might have moved on, he showed up. She placed her feet on the floor and sat on the edge of the bed. His face, thinner than she remembered, was strained and emphasized the dark circles under his eyes. He looked as if he had been dragged through a minefield.

Concern bounced around in her gut as she slowly approached him. Fully clothed, except for his coat and shoes, his hair was mussed, and his normally tanned skin looked paler than she remembered. *How long had he been sleeping like this?* Her heart ached for him. Even in sleep, he looked so tired.

She sat on the edge of the lounger. "Zack." She cupped his warm cheek in her hand and called his name again. Her gaze dropped to his lips. Lips that had brought her more pleasure than shopping at Bloomingdales on a one day doorbuster sale. She hadn't felt his lips against hers in weeks and couldn't resist.

Jada ran the pad of her thumb across his bottom lip, eliciting a twitch from him and bringing a smile to her face. She lowered her head and covered his mouth with hers, lingering, and savoring the moment she'd dreamed about. A shock wave of sensation soared through her body, stirring a passion within her that she hadn't felt in weeks. Oh, how she had missed him, missed this.

Zack responded instantly. "Jada," he mumbled her name against her mouth and braced her face between his hands. His tongue lovingly explored the inner recesses of her mouth as their moans intertwined as one. Jada knew she was home. "Aw, Sweetheart. God I've missed you." He sat forward but cried out in pain. Releasing her suddenly, his head fell against the back of the lounge. His eyes slammed shut, and his face contorted. "*Ah damn! Damn.*" He continued cursing under his breath.

"What? What is it?" She leaped up, wringing her hands. Her heart threatened to beat out of her chest as she shuffled from side to side, unsure of what to do. The agony on his face tore at her insides. "Zack you're scaring me! Please tell me what's wrong."

His jaw tightened, and his hands fisted at his side. The tough man she'd grown to love looked as if he wanted to jump out of his skin. Seconds passed before he finally spoke.

"Jada."

"I'm right here." She reached for his hand, and he stiffened. "Baby tell me what's wrong. What do you need me to do?"

"Spasms … bad. Need … *ah sh…* need a minute." He swallowed hard, his breathing ragged.

She ran to the bathroom for some ibuprofen and water, hoping the medicine would relieve some of the pain. When she returned, his red face covered in a light sheen of perspiration, was clammy to the touch. A cold knot settled in her gut. *This is not good.* She was no stranger to him coming home, muscles tight and his body riddled with pain after a game, but this time seemed worse.

She helped him take a couple of pills, hoping they'd work fast. She left him again to wet a towel and wipe the perspiration from his face. Minutes had passed before he seemed to settle down.

"Why did you sleep in the chair? Why didn't you wake me? You could've slept in the bed." It broke her heart each time he came home, and she witnessed the type of pain he experienced after a game. "Maybe I should get you to the hospital."

"No. I'll be al … alright." He still hadn't opened his eyes, but his breathing seemed to be back to normal.

"You don't look alright. As a matter of fact, you look awful." She wiped at his face again, wishing she could wipe away some of the exhaustion seeping through his pores.

"When was the last time you ate or slept?"

He lifted his eyelids, the blue in his eyes darker than usual. "I could ask you the same questions," he said groggily. His eyes searched hers, and he seemed to want to say more, but hesitated. "We have to talk. Today. Now. Sweetheart, I can't keep living like this. *We* can't keep living like this."

"I know," she whispered. She glanced down at the way his body was angled, knowing that if he didn't get in a bed and stretch out, he was going to be in even more pain later. "Are you able to sit up? You can't stay like this. You need to get in bed."

"There you go, always trying to get me into bed." His eyes were closed, but she didn't miss the humor behind his words.

"Funny. Very funny. If you weren't in so much pain, I'd pop you."

He opened his eyes again, the smile no longer on his lips. "I've missed you so much. I can't live without you. Sweetie, I love you so damn much."

Tears formed in Jada's eyes. Her heart swelled at the sincerity and agony of his words. "I love you too and I'm ready to talk, but not until you get some rest. Let me help you into bed."

***

Hours later Zack opened his eyes to find Jada sitting up in bed next to him, flipping through a magazine. He turned onto his side. Facing her, glad his back spasms were more like a dull ache than a knife slicing through his spine.

"Hi." She tossed the magazine to the other side of the bed and scooted down next to him. "I was starting to wonder if you were going to sleep the day away."

"I feel like I could." His voice raspy. "I haven't slept that sound since you left me."

She visibly swallowed and looked away. Zack was done playing games. He'd given her space to work out whatever was going on with her, but today he wasn't leaving until they hashed out their differences.

"I'm sorry I left the way I did, but I had to get away." Her hand rested against his bare chest. Before climbing into bed earlier, she had helped him strip out of his clothes. The pain that wracked his body then, made him almost consider her offer of going to the hospital. "I was caught off guard by the things Shane said about me."

Zack wrapped his arm around her, pulling her closer and ignoring the twinge in his shoulder. "Sweetheart, I'm so sorry you had to hear or see any of that. But after all the time we've spent together, you have to know how much you mean to me. How much I love you. Don't you?" He lifted her chin so that their eyes could meet. "You do know that I would give up everything I owned to be with you, right?"

She nodded. "I know. But at the time, I couldn't see past the hurt, the ache in my heart. It did get me to thinking, however. I have had time to reevaluate my life, and there are some things you should know."

Zack braced himself. It would kill him if she decided that they couldn't be together.

"Unlike some people who work their butts off in high school in order to get into a great college and then get that dream job, that wasn't me. All of my life my thoughts and actions have always been about *me*. What's in it for *me*?" She blew out a noisy sigh. "My lifelong goal has been to find and marry a rich man. Falling in love was not part of the plan. I just wanted to hook up with someone who could wine and dine me, as well as support my expensive tastes."

Zack didn't speak. He didn't move. In fact, he was barely breathing. When he said they needed to talk, he had no idea the conversation would go in this direction.

"I didn't know I would fall in love with you." She raised up on her elbow and stared down at him. "When I went home after our first date, filthy, exhausted, dehydrated, and in a pair of expensive tennis shoes that were ruined, I hadn't planned on there being a second date. But your kindness, thoughtfulness and compassion had me curious. You were so different than anyone I've ever dated."

If she started talking about her exes, Zack would have to end the conversation. The thought of her with someone else sparked something territorial within him. He didn't even want to think about her in another man's arms.

"The more time I spent with you, the more time I wanted to spend with you. Not because of your amazing home or the fancy cars you drive, and not even because of the new wardrobe you gave me, but because you made me feel special." Her soft hand caressed his face, and Zack swallowed the lump in his throat. "But when Shane said that I was a gold-digger and wasn't good enough for you, I agreed."

"Whoa, Jada." Zack tried to raise up, but she stopped him with a hand on his shoulder.

"Zack let me finish. I started thinking about all that you have accomplished in your life, and how successful you are, and how you have your whole life planned. Then I realized I had nothing to show for my twenty plus years, except expensive clothes, shoes, and overdue credit cards. Baby, I have nothing to contribute to our relationship. I have nothing to offer you."

"Okay, that's enough." Zack sat up, ignoring the popping of his bones and the ache throughout his whole body. "I can't listen to this anymore."

"I'm sorry. I'll understand if you want nothing else to do with me." Tears filled her pretty brown eyes, and she moved away from him. "But please know that I love you."

"Wait." He gently grabbed hold of her arm and pulled her back. "We're not done here. First of all, you have no reason to be sorry. So what if you have always dreamed of having the finer things in life. Most of us have. As for the expensive clothes and credit card debt, I happen to like you in your expensive clothes, especially your sexy underwear." He wiggled his eyebrows, and she laughed. "Don't worry about the credit cards, we'll take care of them … and then cut them up." He turned serious and framed her face in his hands, forcing her to look into his eyes. "I need you to listen to what I'm about to say. Don't *ever* think that you're not good enough for me. Sweetheart, you are the best thing that has ever happened to me. I wake up in the morning thinking of you and go to bed wishing you were there with me. I wasn't kidding this morning when I said that I couldn't keep living like this. I can't live without you. I will *not* live without you!"

He reached for his pants at the foot of the bed and dug through the pockets. Pulling out a small velvet box that he had been carrying around for weeks, he opened it. "I would get down on my knees for this, but please don't make me."

Jada laughed. Tears streamed down her cheeks faster than she could wipe them away.

"Your Highness, I promise to treat you like the queen that you are. I will keep your closet and drawers full of sexy clothes and underwear. And I will love you until the day I die if you agree to marry me."

"Oh my God, yes. I'll marry you," she cried. Her arms draped around his neck as she peppered his face with kisses. "I love you so much."

EPILOGUE

Two months later.

"Ohhh, he's so cute."

"Move, I can't see him."

"Let me hold him."

Everyone spoke at once, as they crowded in Toni's hospital room, welcoming Craig Junior into the world. Jada didn't know who was happier for the newest Jenkins addition, the parents or the grandparents, aunts, uncles, and cousins. The hospital staff had warned them they couldn't all be in the room at the same time, but saying no to Katherine Jenkins wasn't easy. Her gramma sweetly asked that her family be allowed fifteen minutes in the room to see the baby and pray together as a family. The hospital agreed to seven minutes.

"All right everyone. Time to go," the nurse said. "I can allow one or two of you in here at a time, but the rest of you must head to the waiting room."

"Congratulations, girl," Jada said, hugging Toni. "I'm so happy for you and Craig. Little Craig is absolutely beautiful."

"Thank you guys." Toni accepted a hug from Zack. "Thanks for coming. I'm so glad to see the two of you together. All of this," she waved her hand, "will be you one day."

Zack wrapped his arm around Jada's shoulder and placed a kiss against her temple. "Definitely." Zack beamed. They had talked about having two or three children, but not until they were married a year and did some traveling.

They left the room followed by the rest of the Jenkins clan, and Jada's heart felt as if it would explode with excitement. She couldn't ever remember being as happy as she'd been lately. The last couple of months with Zack had been like a dream come true. They were getting into a daily rhythm. He had officially retired from the NFL and spent much of his time volunteering at a local Boys and Girls Club. Jada hadn't moved in with him, but considering how often she was at his house, she might as well have. The long drive to work bugged her, but most days Zack drove her and then picked her up.

When the whole family was back in the waiting room, Jada and Zack said their goodbyes before leaving the hospital. They were scheduled to visit a few potential wedding venues that afternoon, as well as a bakery for cake tasting. Jada had dreamed about her ideal wedding for so long. Now that she was getting what she wanted, it didn't seem real.

"Hey, you guys, wait up." Christina chased after them. "Can you drop me off at the airport?"

"Yeah, sure." Zack opened the front and back passenger doors, before rounding the truck and climbing into the driver's seat. "So where are you off to this weekend?"

"She's going to see *Luke*," Jada said in a sing-song voice, giggling when her cousin popped her in the back of the head. Her cousin's secret life was also taking her to New York more often, and seeing Luke was working in her favor when it came to not telling the family what she was really up to.

Jada would never betray her cousin's confidence, but she hoped Christina came clean soon with the family. In the meantime, Jada would play along. "I don't know why you're keeping things hush, hush about Luke. We all know you two are an item."

The three of them kept a steady stream of conversation going until Zack dropped Christina at the airport. Two hours later, he pulled his Land Rover onto the Ravenwood Castle property. Jada had heard about the estate but wasn't prepared for the majestic surroundings and the medieval flair of the buildings.

"This is … wow," were the only words she could form to describe their surroundings.

Zack shut off the vehicle, undid his seat belt, and turned to her. "What's on your mind?" He reached for her hand and kissed the back of it. "You've barely said two words since we dropped off CJ. You make me nervous when you get quiet."

Jada smiled and undid her seat belt. "I've been thinking."

"Oh boy. Every time you start thinking—"

"Zack!" She punched him in the arm, and he rubbed the offended appendage in mock pain. "I'm serious."

Laughing he said, "Okay, sweetheart. I'm sorry." He pulled her to him for a kiss, his hand at the back of her neck. "Tell me what's on your mind."

"I'm thinking about going back to school."

"Really? What will you major in?"

"I'm thinking either fashion or business. I'd like to be a buyer, a fashion buyer someday. What do you think?"

He massaged the back of her neck, something she was quickly growing accustomed to and loving every minute of his gentle caress.

"I think it's a great idea as long as you're going back to school because you want to, not because you think me or anyone else expects you to continue your education." He continued to study her. "I have a feeling there's something else on your mind. What is it? What's bothering you?"

She smiled and shook her head. It was getting to the point that she couldn't hide anything from him, but she had no complaints. She loved that he was so in tuned with her.

"How would you feel if we didn't get married in a church or a castle?" She glanced at the main building, loving how authentic it looked despite not being a real hundred-year-old castle.

"Hold up." Zack leaned back, his dark eyebrows slanted in a frown. "Is this a trick question? Some of my married friends warned me that you might throw out trick questions occasionally. Like, do these jeans make me look fat? Or are my hips too big?"

Jada threw her head back and burst out laughing. She could just picture Craig or one of Zack's former teammates telling him that. "No, I'm serious. I've been thinking about all of the wedding planning lately. The decisions that have to be made, the cost, just … all of it. What do you think about us eloping?"

"Sweetheart, I will marry you anytime and anywhere, but I want to make sure you have the type of wedding day you've been dreaming of. You know you don't have to worry about the money, and you don't have to plan everything yourself. That's what wedding planners or mothers are for. But most importantly, what about the fantasy? I thought you wanted the long flowing dress and wanted to get married in a castle?"

"Well." She stared down at their joined hands, remembering their first date and how much she'd grown since then. Gazing into his crystal blue eyes, she felt that she had everything she'd ever wanted. "Zack," she cupped his cheek, loving the feel of the scruff along his jawline. "I have plenty of long flowing dresses and your home is like a castle. Most importantly, I'm engaged to the man of my dreams. Technically, the fantasy has almost been fulfilled. Once we say 'I do'," she shrugged, "my fantasy will be a reality."

"Well, damn, when you put it that way. Where do you want to go? Hawaii? Bali? Tahiti? Name it, and I will make the arrangements today. We can be out of here first thing in the morning."

Jada laughed. "Wow, you're not wasting any time. I didn't mean we had to leave like … now!"

He stared lovingly into her eyes. "Sweetheart, I have waited a lifetime for you. I don't want to wait any longer." He kissed her forehead, and then her nose, and finally, he settled against her mouth, kissing her as if his life depended on making her happy. The slow, drugging kiss was like none they had ever shared before. Her pulse pounded, and desire roared through her body, igniting the passion waiting to be released. Oh yeah, this was what she wanted to look forward to for the rest of her life.

Breathing heavy she gripped his face. "Okay, okay, uh, how about Vegas?"

The End

If you enjoyed this book by Sharon C. Cooper,
please consider leaving a review on any online book site,
review site, or social media outlet.

ABOUT THE AUTHOR

Bestselling author, Sharon C. Cooper, spent 10 years as a sheet metal worker. And while enjoying that unique line of work, she attended college in the evening and obtained her B.A. from Concordia University in Business Management with an emphasis in Communication. Sharon is a romance-a-holic - loving anything that involves romance with a happily-ever-after, whether in books, movies or real life. She writes contemporary romance, as well as romantic suspense and enjoys rainy days, carpet picnics, and peanut butter and jelly sandwiches. When Sharon is not writing or working, she's hanging out with her amazing husband, doing volunteer work or reading a good book (a romance of course). To read more about Sharon and her novels, visit:

Website: http://sharoncooper.net
Facebook:
http://www.facebook.com/AuthorSharonCCooper21?ref=hl
Twitter: https://twitter.com/#!/Sharon_Cooper1
Subscribe to her blog: http://sharonccooper.wordpress.com/
Goodreads:
http://www.goodreads.com/author/show/5823574.Sharon_C
_Cooper

OTHER TITLES BY SHARON C. COOPER:

Jenkins Family Series (Contemporary Romance)
Best Woman for the Job (Short Story Prequel)
Still the Best Woman for the Job (book 1)
All You'll Ever Need (book 2)
Tempting the Artist (book 3) – *Coming Soon*
Negotiating for Love – (book 4) – *Coming Soon*
Seducing the Boss Lady – (book 5) – *Coming Soon*

Reunited Series (Romantic Suspense)
Blue Roses (book 1)
Secret Rendezvous (Prequel to Rendezvous with Danger)
Rendezvous with Danger (book 2)
Truth or Consequences (book 3)
Book 4 (Wiz's story) – *Coming Soon*
Book 5 (Hunter's story) – *Coming Soon*

Stand Alones
Something New ("Edgy" Sweet Romance)
Legal Seduction
(Harlequin Kimani – Contemporary Romance)
Sin City Temptation
(Harlequin Kimani – Contemporary Romance)
coming March 2015
A Dose of Passion
(Harlequin Kimani – Contemporary Romance)
coming October 2015

STILL THE BEST WOMAN FOR THE JOB
(TONI & CRAIG'S STORY)

EXCERPT

"Would you come on," Toni Jenkins gasped for air. "Put your back into it, Jada. How can you lug sheet metal around all day and can't help drag a sloppy drunk to the bathroom?"

Jada's chest heaved and her long, dark hair whipped across her face. She glared around Ronald's body at Toni. "Say one more thing and I will drop his heavy ass right here in the middle of the hallway. Then see how far you get in hiding him. Grampa's going to kill you when he finds out you're hanging out with drunks and that you brought one of them to his birthday party!"

Toni clamped her mouth shut and pulled the hem of her short dress down with one hand while she held onto her date, Ronald, with her other. She needed Jada's help. The last thing she wanted is for her grandmother to find out Ronald barfed on an eight-foot Golden Cane Palm Tree, one of her prize possessions. No, she couldn't handle a lecture tonight, but if her grandfather got wind of the night's events, that's exactly what she would get. *Character is built by the choices we make,* her grandfather's familiar words taunted.

"Wha … what are yo … you doin' to me," Ronald slurred before his head dipped to the side and a low snore rumbled against Toni's ear.

"Oh, shut up," she mumbled under her breath.

What did her recent dating choices say about her character? Ronald might have been tall, good-looking and possessed a body women fantasized about, but he wasn't the brightest bulb on the Christmas tree. If she were honest with herself, she'd have to admit that she'd dated her share of losers since breaking up with Craig.

Argh! Why can't I stop thinking about him?

As soon as the question leaped into her mind, so did the answer. She was still in love with Craig Logan … and she hated it. *Okay, stop thinking about him. Don't think about him, don't think about—* "Oh crap." Toni grabbed hold of the nearby wall when her foot slipped and she lost her grip on Ronald.

Her cousin glared at her. "If you don't…" she started but didn't finish when Toni regained her footing and grasped the back of Ronald's shirt, bringing him upright again. Thankfully, the bathroom was in sight and none of the party guest had found their way to the back of the house. The area was empty and quiet, perfect for hiding a body.

When they finally wrangled Ronald into the bathroom, both she and Jada collapsed against the cool, marbled tiled wall, Ronald's limp body propped up between them.

"Just think, only a Jenkins' girl could pull a two hundred pound man from a crowded ballroom and drag him through Gramma and Grampa's house wearing cocktail dresses and stilettos without anyone being the wiser," Jada wheezed.

"You're right." Toni closed her eyes, breathing heavily.

Thanks to their grandfather for encouraging her and her female cousins to pursue a career in the construction trades, Toni was now a master plumber. A career in plumbing seemed like the perfect solution after dropping out of college. Not only had she finished her apprenticeship five years ago, but she had also attended night school to complete her degree in mechanical engineering.

"I know this is a fine time to ask, but why did we bring him into the bathroom instead of dumping his butt in the backyard until he sobers up?"

Toni glanced at the bathroom door thinking she should probably close it, but was too tired to move. "We can't just chuck him outside and leave him. Hopefully he'll come to, but in the meantime, I need to clean him up so we can put him in the car and take him home."

"*We*?" Jada's voice raised an octave. She moved away from the wall but stopped when Ronald's body started sliding. "You are crazy in your head if you think I'm dragging him anywhere else! Look at me." With a flourish of her free hand, she brought attention to her short, Michael Kors dress. "Do you have any idea how much I paid for this outfit? I'm not about to let some boneheaded drunk throw up on me. I say we dump his butt on the floor and go get Johnny and the guys to throw him in the back of one of their trucks."

Toni liked the idea, but didn't know where her male cousins were hiding out. She hadn't seen them since they'd showed up at the party, late. It was safe to assume they were somewhere watching a basketball game since the NBA finals had just started.

"Okay, let's slowly slide his body down the wall and onto the floor." Toni bent her knees and they eased him along the tile, which wasn't easy to do in stilettos and a tight dress. "Almost there just … oh no! Jada grab him!" Too late. Ronald's body jerked, Toni's arms flailed and the three of them crashed to the floor in a heap.

"Aaarrrgh!" Jada shrieked. Caramel toned arms and legs flapped around in distress under the weight of Ronald's body sprawled on top of Jada, his boozed breath in her face. "Oh my God! Oh my God! Get him off me! I think he just drooled on my dress," she screamed. "Toni, I'm going to kill you!"

***

Craig Logan pulled up to the Jenkins' family estate, a colossal brick home that expanded half the block located in the Village of Indian Hill, a suburb of Cincinnati. A mere representation of the Jenkins's wealth, the house stood out with every light shining through the cathedral style windows and illuminated the sky like fireworks on the fourth of July. Craig's fingers gripped the steering wheel tighter, and he willed the mounting anxiousness in his gut to loosen up. Knowing he'd see Toni soon brought mixed feelings. On one hand, he couldn't wait to see her, but on the other he wasn't sure he wanted to put himself through the torture of seeing her without being able to hold her in his arms.

He pulled onto the property. Luxury cars lined either side of the circular driveway that easily accommodated fifty cars. It wasn't until he noticed vehicles lining the paved driveway along the side of the house that he knew this was no small gathering, but what had he expected? The Jenkins family, well known across the state of Ohio, had probably invited everybody who's anybody to the celebration.

He parked his car at the very end of the driveway, but didn't make a move to exit the vehicle still unsure of whether or not showing up was a good idea. When Toni's cousin, Peyton, insisted on him stopping by, saying how much the family had missed seeing him, he thought attending the party was a good idea. But now, he wasn't so sure.

His cell phone rang and he slowly dug the iPhone out of his pocket, debating on whether or not to answer. He was already late, and it wouldn't take much for him to change his mind about the party despite the fact that he'd driven forty-five minutes to get there.

He glanced at the cell phone screen and smiled. "Hello."

"What's up bro?"

"Hey man, what's going on?"

The sound of his brother's voice was a welcomed

distraction. Two years older, Derek was more than his big brother he was also his best friend.

"Not too much, did I catch you at a bad time?" Derek asked.

"Actually I was just sitting here trying to force myself to go into Toni's grandfather's birthday celebration."

"Oh yeah, I forgot that was tonight. Why were you debating whether or not to go in? You already told Peyton you would be there and besides, I know you want to see Toni."

Craig traced the ridged lines on the steering wheel with his index finger, going in and out of the grooves thinking about the night he and Toni parted ways. *I can't handle dating a cop*, she had told him through her tears. *That could have been you.*

Craig and his partner of three years were both shot during a domestic violence call. He survived, but his partner hadn't. Craig would never forget that hot summer night, neighbors screaming and blood everywherc. It wasn't until he was lying in a hospital bed, with Toni by his side that his sergeant told him Julien hadn't survived. Craig remembered holding Toni in his arms providing as much comfort to her as he could offer, considering he had just lost one of his best friends.

"You're right," he finally said to his brother, "I do want to see her, but I don't know if I can handle being that close to her and then just walk away afterwards." He used his familiar I'm-in-control voice, but at this moment nothing was further from the truth.

"So you're still in love with her?" his brother asked.

"You know I am." Craig toyed with the car keys that dangled from the ignition. He thought dating other women would take his mind off Toni. If anything, dating others made him want her that much more.

"Well, I guess you know what you have to do." His brother's voice permeated his thoughts.

Craig kneaded the tight knot that formed between his eyes. "And what's that?"

"Give up the badge."

He dropped his hand and pounded the steering wheel. "Damn, Derek, you act as if sacrificing my career is easy." The knot in his stomach tightened. There wasn't much he wouldn't do for Toni, but what he did for a living meant so much more than just carrying a badge.

"Being willing to sacrifice your career is easy if Toni means as much to you as you say she does. Craig, it's not like you're hurting for money. When Uncle Sammy left you that house and enough money to do whatever the hell you wanted, I thought you would quit the force then."

Craig tensed in his seat. "Being a cop is not about the money and you know it! I shouldn't have to give up a job I love and one that I'm damn good at because Toni's afraid I might die in the line of duty."

Derek hesitated. "Are you sure that's why you're still on the force? Or are you still fighting those demons? Trying to rid the streets of every single thug, whose goal in life is to attack and rape defenseless women."

Craig gripped his cell phone tighter and clenched his jaw as he willed himself not to react to his brother's words. Since the night he'd received the phone call that his fiancée had been raped and killed, he vowed to do everything in his power to make sure it didn't happen to any other woman. And then when he met Toni and found out she had gone through a similar experience in college, his being a cop took on a whole different meaning. He had to do whatever he could do to protect the female population from bastards who thought they had a right to abuse women.

"Listen, I'm not trying to piss you off, but I think it's time you realize that you are just one man. As sick as this reality may be, there will always be some butthole running the streets with evil intent. You can't stop or catch them all."

Craig rolled his shoulders and took a cleansing breath. He

knew he couldn't stop them all, but he sure as hell could try.

"Hey, I didn't call to preach to you, but I did call to see if Jason and I could stay with you for a few days."

Craig's mood lightened at the mention of his three-year-old nephew, of whom his brother had sole custody. "You know you don't have to ask. You guys are always welcome."

"Good. We need a break from the renovations. The contractors have finished the upstairs bathroom, and now started on the kitchen. I can't take the chaos anymore."

Craig chuckled. "I warned you that remodeling was going to be a pain. I'm surprised you lasted this long. You and my nephew can stay as long as you need to."

Growing up in Columbus, Craig knew he didn't want to live there all his life, so when Derek relocated to Cincinnati, he did too. They now lived about twenty-five minutes from each other and hung out as often as possible.

"Great. I'm thinking we'll get there Wednesday and stay a few days or a week at the longest."

"Sounds good to me. Stay as long as you want."

"And Craig …"

"Yeah."

"Go to the party. Toni's missing you probably as much as you're missing her. Besides, if she's there, I'm sure she'll do something or has done something that will require you to bail her out of a situation." His brother laughed and then ended the call.

Craig grinned. Derek was right. Toni did have a way of getting herself into tight jams.

***

Toni chuckled as she tugged on one of Ronald's arms, at first unable to budge him off her cousin, but eventually rolling him away, just enough for Jada to scurry from under him. Toni crawled to the side and clamped her hand on the edge of the claw-foot tub for support as she laughed outright, barely able to catch her breath. If there were any witnesses to the last ten minutes of her eventful evening, they'd be rolling on the floor laughing.

She turned her head slightly to see Jada sitting against the vanity, wiping her eyes and laughing too. Her expensive dress hiked up and barely covering her most precious gift, looked as if it had been trampled. Toni knew that if her cousin had a clue of how disheveled her hair was, she would be out for blood.

"How is it that I always get roped into messes like this whenever I'm anywhere near you?" Jada rested her head against the wall. "Please. Tell me why this always happens."

Still on her knees, Toni rested her forehead against the coolness of the tub not caring how crazy she probably looked. All she needed was a couple of minutes to regroup. "It doesn't *always* happen. Besides, you should be thanking me that I bring excitement and variety to your life."

"Girl, please. I have enough excitement and variety in my life. It's you who needs to get her act together and stop dating these jerks. I think MJ was right the other night. At some point you need to ask yourself, 'When am I going to stop dating these losers?'"

Toni lifted her head and glared at her cousin. "Not all of my dates are losers, and I don't appreciate you two talking about me behind my back. I'm sure there are more interesting subjects to discuss than my social life." Granted some of her choices in men as of late were questionable, but that was nobody's business but hers. "And another thing, how is MJ going to talk about who anyone dates when all she does is stomp on the pride of every man she comes in contact with and treat them like crap?"

Toni loved all of her cousins, but Martina (MJ) Jenkins lack of tact and straight-talk-no-chaser attitude was enough to make you want to slug her sometime. Five years older than Toni, Martina made it a point to try to school them all on why men were the lowest form of human life and how they were only good for sex and at times, according to Martina, weren't that good at that.

"Hey don't get mad at us because you keep picking boneheads." She waved a hand in Ronald's direction. "It's not like you can't do better. You're smart, have a good job, and you're cute – but not as cute as me," she flipped her dark hair over her shoulder, then glanced down at her dress and adjusted the thin shoulder straps. "Girl, you're a Jenkins. A proud, educated black woman who can do anything you set your mind to do. You might as well face it. Ever since you broke up with cutie-pie Craig Logan, you have been scraping the bottom of the barrel for male companionship. Your drunk boyfriend is proof. You can continue to be in denial if you want, but until you get yourself together, we're going to keep talking about you."

"What?" Toni turned slightly, still gripping the edge of the tub. "What are you talking about? I'm not in denial about anything. I have not—"

"Ahem."

All talk ceased. Toni was almost afraid to look back to see who had cleared their throat. There were two people she didn't want to see when she turned around - her grandfather or her pain-in-the butt cousin, MJ. Either one of them would make her feel worse than she already did about bringing Ronald to the party. *I knew I should have closed that damn door.*

Blowing out a frustrated breath she slowly turned her head toward the door and the steady thump of her heart went haywire. Heat soared to every cell in her body when her gaze met clear, hazel eyes that twinkled with mirth and belonged to the tall, gorgeous specimen whose broad shoulders were almost as wide as the bathroom doorway. *Craig.*

"Please tell me that guy isn't dead and that I don't have to arrest you two for murder."

Buy now from all major online retailers
http://www.sharoncooper.net/

Printed in the USA
CPSIA information can be obtained
at www.ICGtesting.com
LVHW010444060624
782430LV00001B/78

9 780990 350538